Praise for Charles D'Ambrosio's
THE POINT

"However wrecked the lives in these stories, they are deeply felt
and beautifully rendered; as stories, in fact, they're nearly perfect."
— *Men's Journal*

"I love these stories, this voice of Charles D'Ambrosio's which
spins out long, complex, involving scenarios, no two alike, but
all of them clearly the work of a single sensibility. He writes
with such intelligence — a moral as well as a verbal intelligence — that he reminds me of a generation of short story
writers that did not want to pare down experience . . . but
rather to enrich it, contemplate its paradoxes, *think about it*
on the page."
— Rosellen Brown, author of *Before and After*

"Charles D'Ambrosio brings large ambitions and a versatile tal-
ent to the short story form; whether in the tightly focused,
gemlike "The Point" — one of the best stories I've read in years —
or in the muscular, long-distance narratives like "Her Real
Name" and "Jacinta," he proves himself a significant new
American voice."
— Jay McInerney

THE POINT

AND OTHER STORIES

CHARLES D'AMBROSIO

LITTLE, BROWN AND COMPANY

BOSTON   NEW YORK   TORONTO   LONDON

First Paperback Edition

Grateful acknowledgment is made to the following publications in which some of
these stories were first published: *The New Yorker*, "The Point"; *The Paris Review*,
"Her Real Name" and "Open House"; *Story*, "Jacinta" and "January" (the second
part of "Lyricism," previously titled "A Christmas Card"); *The Cimarron Review*,
"All Aboard."

Several of these stories have been reprinted in the following anthologies: "The Point,"
Best American Short Stories 1991, edited by Alice Adams and Katrina Kenison, and
I Know Some Things: Stories About Childhood, edited by Lorrie Moore; "Her Real
Name," *Voices of the Xiled*, edited by Mike Wexler, and *The Penguin Book of New
American Writing*, edited by Jay McInerney; "Jacinta," *The Pushcart Anthology*.

Library of Congress Cataloging-in-Publication Data

D'Ambrosio, Charles.
    The point : and other stories / Charles D'Ambrosio. — 1st ed.
        p.   cm.
    Contents: The point — Her real name — American bullfrog —
Jacinta — All aboard — Lyricism — Open house.
    ISBN 0-316-17144-1 (hc) 0-316-17125-5 (pb)
    1. United States — Social life and customs — 20th century — Fiction.
I. Title.
PS3554.A469P65 1995
813'.54 — dc20   94-25170

10 9 8 7 6 5 4 3 2 1

MV-NY

*Published simultaneously in Canada
by Little, Brown & Company (Canada) Limited*

Printed in the United States of America

For Elisabeth Robinson

THE AUTHOR wishes to thank James Michener and the Copernicus Society of America, the Henfield Foundation, and the Institute of Creative Writing at the University of Wisconsin for their support. For their dedication to writing in general, and to my work in particular, I would also like to thank my friends Tom Grimes and Chris Hallman; my agent, Mary Evans; and my editor, Jordan Pavlin.

CONTENTS

THE POINT

THE POINT

I HAD BEEN lying awake after my nightmare, a nightmare in which Father and I bought helium balloons at a circus. I tied mine around my finger and Father tied his around a stringbean and lost it. After that, I lay in the dark, tossing and turning, sleepless from all the sand in my sheets and all the uproar out in the living room. Then the door opened, and for a moment the blade of bright light blinded me. The party was still going full blast, and now with the door ajar and my eyes adjusting I glimpsed the silver smoke swirling in the light and all the people suspended in it, hovering around as if they were angels in Heaven — some kind of Heaven where the host serves highballs and the men smoke cigars and the women all smell like rotting fruit. Everything was hysterical out there — the men laughing, the ice clinking, the women shrieking. A woman crossed over and sat on the edge of my bed, bending over me. It was Mother. She was backlit, a vague, looming silhouette, but I could smell lily of the valley and something else — lemon rind from the bitter twist she always chewed when she reached the watery bottom of her vodka-and-tonic. When Father was alive, she rarely drank, but after he shot himself you could say she really let herself go.

"Dearest?" she said.

"Hi, Mom," I said.

"Your old mother's bombed, dearest — flat-out bombed."

"That's okay," I said. She liked to confess these things to me, although it was always obvious how tanked she was, and I never cared. I considered myself a pro at this business. "It's a party," I said, casually. "Live it up."

"Oh, God," she laughed. "I don't know how I got this way."

"What do you want, Mom?"

"Yes, dear," she said. "There was something I wanted."

She looked out the window — at the sail-white moon beyond the black branches of the apple tree — and then she looked into my eyes. "What was it I wanted?" Her eyes were moist, and mapped with red veins. "I came here for a reason," she said, "but I've forgotten it now."

"Maybe if you go back you'll remember," I suggested.

Just then, Mrs. Gurney leaned through the doorway. "Well?" she said, slumping down on the floor. Mrs. Gurney had bright-silver hair and a dark tan — the sort of tan that women around here get when their marriages start busting up. I could see the gaudy gold chains looped around Mrs. Gurney's dark-brown neck winking in the half-light before they plunged from sight into the darker gulf between her breasts.

"That's it," Mother said. "Mrs. Gurney. She's worse off than me. She's really blitzo. Blotto? Blitzed?"

"Hand me my jams," I said.

I slipped my swim trunks on underneath the covers. For years, I'd been escorting these old inebriates over the sandy playfield and along the winding boardwalks and up the salt-whitened steps of their homes, brewing coffee, fixing a little toast or heating leftovers, searching the medicine cabinets for aspirin and Vitamin B, setting a glass of water on the nightstand, or the coffee table if they'd collapsed on the couch — and even, once, tucking some old fart snugly into bed between purple silk sheets. I'd guide these drunks home and hear stories about the alma mater, Theta Xi, Boeing stock splits, Cadillacs, divorce, Nembutal, infidelity, and often the people I helped home gave me three or four bucks for listening to all their sad business. I suppose it was better than a paper route. Father, who'd been a medic in Vietnam, made it my job when I was ten, and at thirteen I considered myself a hard-core veteran, treating every trip like a mission.

"Okay, Mrs. Gurney," I said. "Upsy-daisy."

She held her hand out, and I grabbed it, leaned back, and hoisted her to her feet. She stood there a minute, listing this way, that way, like a sailor who hadn't been to port in a while.

Mother kissed her wetly on the lips and then said to me, "Hurry home."

"I'm toasted," Mrs. Gurney explained. "Just toasted."

"Let's go out the back way," I said. It would only take longer if we had to navigate our way through the party, offering excuses and making those ridiculous promises adults always make to one another when the party's over. "Hey, we'll do it again," they assure each other, as if that needed to be said. And I'd noticed how, with the summer ending, and Labor Day approaching, all the adults would acquire a sort of desperate, clinging manner, as if this were all going to end forever, and the good times would never be seen again. Of course I now realize that the end was just an excuse to party like maniacs. The softball tournament, the salmon derby, the cocktails, the clambakes, the barbecues would all happen again. They always had and they always would.

Anyway, out the back door and down the steps.

Once, I'd made a big mistake with a retired account executive, a friend of Father's. Fred was already falling-down drunk, so it didn't help at all that he had two more drinks on the way out the door, apologizing for his condition, which no one noticed, and boisterously offering bad stock tips. I finally got Fred going and dragged him partway home in a wagon, dumping his fat ass in front of his house — close enough, I figured — wedged in against some driftwood so the tide wouldn't wash him out to sea. He didn't get taken out to sea, but the sea did come to him, as the tide rose, and when he woke he was lassoed in green kelp. Fortunately, he'd forgotten the whole thing — how he'd got where he was, where he'd been before that — but it scared me, that a more or less right-hearted attempt on my part might end in such an ugly mess.

By now, though, I'd worked this job so long I knew all the tricks.

The moon was full and immaculately white in a blue-black sky. The wind funneled down Saratoga Passage, blowing hard, blowing south, and Mrs. Gurney and I were struggling against it, tacking back and forth across the playfield. Mrs. Gurney strangled her arm around my neck and we wobbled along. Bits of sand shot in our eyes and blinded us.

"Keep your head down, Mrs. Gurney! I'll guide you!"

She plopped herself down in the sand, nesting there as if she were going to lay an egg. She unbuckled her sandals and tossed them behind her. I ran back and fetched them from the sand. Her skirt fluttered in the wind and flew up in her face. Her silver hair, which was usually shellacked with spray and coiffed to resemble a crash helmet, cracked and blew apart, splintering like a clutch of straw.

"Why'd I drink so damned much?" she screamed. "I'm toasted — really, Kurt, I'm totally toasted. I shouldn't have drunk so damn much."

"Well, you did, Mrs. Gurney," I said, bending toward her. "That's not the problem now. The problem now is how to get you home."

"Why, God damn it!"

"Trust me, Mrs. Gurney. Home is where you want to be."

One tip about these drunks: My opinion is that it pays in the long run to stick as close as possible to the task at hand. We're just going home, you assure them, and tomorrow it will all be different. I've found if you stray too far from the simple goal of getting home and going to sleep you let yourself in for a lot of unnecessary hell. You start hearing about their whole miserable existence, and suddenly it's the most important thing in the world to fix it all up, right then. Certain things in life can't be repaired, as in Father's situation, and that's always sad, but I believe there's nothing in life that can be remedied under the influence of half a dozen planter's punches.

Now, not everyone on the Point was a crazed rumhound, but the ones that weren't, the people who accurately assessed their capacities and balanced their intake accordingly, the people who never got lost, who never passed out in flower beds or, adrift in the maze of narrow boardwalks, gave up the search for home altogether and walked into any old house that was nearby — they, the people who never did these things and knew what they were about, never needed my help. They also weren't too friendly with my mother and didn't participate in her weekly bashes. The Point was kind of divided that way — between the upright, seaworthy residents and the easily overturned friends of my mother's.

Mrs. Gurney lived about a half mile up the beach in a bungalow with a lot of Gothic additions. The scuttlebutt on Mrs. Gurney was that while she wasn't divorced, her husband didn't love her. This kind of knowledge was part of my job, something I didn't relish but accepted as an occupational hazard. I knew all the gossip, the rumors, the rising and falling fortunes of my mother's friends. After a summer, I'd have the dirt on everyone, whether I wanted it or not. But I had developed a priestly sense of my position, and whatever anyone told me in a plastered, blathering confessional fit was as safe and privileged as if it had been spoken in a private audience with the Pope. Still, I hoped Mrs. Gurney would stick to the immediate goal and not start talking about how sad and lonely she was, or how cruel her husband was, or what was going to become of us all, etc.

The wind rattled the swings back and forth, chains creaking, and whipped the ragged flag, which flew at half-mast. Earlier that summer, Mr. Crutchfield, the insurance lawyer, had fallen overboard and drowned while hauling in his crab trap. He always smeared his bait box with Mentholatum, which is illegal, and the crabs went crazy for it, and I imagined that in his greed, catching over the limit, he couldn't haul the trap up but wouldn't let go, either, and the weight pulled him into the sea, and he had a heart attack and drowned. The current floated him all the way to Everett before he was found, white and bloated as soggy bread.

Mrs. Gurney was squatting on the ground, lifting fistfuls of sand and letting them course through her fingers, the grains falling away as through an hourglass.

"Mrs. Gurney? We're not making much progress."

She rose to her feet, gripping my pant leg, my shirt, my sleeve, then my neck. We started walking again. The sand was deep and loose, and with every step we sank down through the soft layers until a solid purchase was gained in the hard-packed sand below, and we could push off in baby steps. The night was sharp and alive with shadows — everything, even the tiny tufted weeds that sprouted through the sand, had a shadow — and this deepened the world, made it seem thicker, with layers, and more layers, and then a darkness into which I couldn't see.

"You know," Mrs. Gurney said, "the thing about these parties is, the thing about drinking is — you know, getting so damnably blasted is . . ." She stopped, and tried to mash her wild hair back down into place, and, no longer holding on to anything other than her head, fell back on her ass into the sand.

I waited for her to finish her sentence, then gave up, knowing it was gone forever. Her lipstick, I noticed, was smeared clownishly around her mouth, fixing her lips into a frown, or maybe a smirk. She smelled different from my mother — like pepper, I thought, and bananas. She was taller than me, and a little plump, with a nose shaped exactly like her head, like a miniature replica of it, really, stuck right in the middle of her face.

We finally got off the playfield and onto the boardwalk that fronted the seawall. A wooden wagon leaned over in the sand. I tipped it upright.

"Here you go, Mrs. Gurney," I said, pointing to the wagon. "Hop aboard."

"I'm okay," she protested. "I'm fine. Fine and dandy."

"You're not fine, Mrs. Gurney."

The caretaker built these wagons out of old hatches from P.T. boats. They were heavy, monstrous, and made to last. Once you got them rolling, they cruised.

Mrs. Gurney got in, not without a good deal of operatics, and when I finally got her to shut up and sit down I started pulling. I'd never taken her home before, but on a scale of one to ten, ten being the most obstreperous, I was rating her about a six at this point.

She stretched out like Cleopatra floating down the

Nile in her barge. "Stop the world," she sang, "I want to get off."

I vaguely recalled that as a song from my parents' generation. It reminded me of my father, who shot himself in the head one morning — did I already say this? He was sitting in the grass parking lot above the Point. Officially, his death was ruled an accident, a "death by misadventure," and everyone believed that he had in fact been cleaning his gun, but Mother told me otherwise, one night. Mother had a batch of lame excuses she tried on me, but it only made me sad to see her groping for an answer and falling way short. I wished she'd come up with something, just for herself. Father used to say that everyone up here was *dinky dow*, which is Vietnamese patois for "crazy." At times, after Father died, I thought Mother was going a little *dinky dow* herself.

I leaned forward, my head bent against the wind. Off to starboard, the sea was black, with a line of moonlit white waves continually crashing on the shore. Far off, I could see the dark headlands of Hat Island, the island itself rising from the water like a breaching whale, and then, beyond, the soft, blue, irresolute lights of Everett, on the distant mainland.

I stopped for a breather, and Mrs. Gurney was gone. She was sitting on the boardwalk, a few houses back.

"Look at all these houses," Mrs. Gurney said, swinging her arms around.

"Let's go, Mrs. Gurney."

"Another fucking great summer at the Point."

The wind seemed to be refreshing Mrs. Gurney, but

that was a hard one to call. Often, drunks seemed on the verge of sobering up, and then, just as soon as they got themselves nicely balanced, they plunged off the other side, into depression.

"Poor Crutchfield," Mrs. Gurney said. We stood in front of Mr. Crutchfield's house. An upstairs light — in the bedroom, I knew — was on, although the lower stories were dark and empty. "And Lucy — God, such grief. They loved each other, Kurt." Mrs. Gurney frowned. "They loved each other. And now?"

Actually, the Crutchfields hadn't loved each other — information I alone was privy to. Lucy's grief, I was sure, had to do with the fact that her husband died in a state of absolute misery, and now she would never be able to change things. In Lucy's mind, he would be forever screwing around, and she would be forever waiting for him to cut it out and come home. After he died, she spread the myth of their reconciliation, and everyone believed it, but I knew it to be a lie. Mr. Crutchfield's sense of failure over the marriage was enormous. He blamed himself, as perhaps he should have. But I remember, one night earlier in the summer, telling him it was okay, that if he was unhappy with Lucy, it was fine to fuck around. He said, You think so? I said, Sure, go for it.

Of course, you might ask, what did I know? At thirteen, I'd never even smooched with a girl, but I had nothing to lose by encouraging him. He was drunk, he was miserable, and I had a job, and that job was to get him home and try to prevent him from dwelling too much on himself.

It was that night, the night I took Mr. Crutchfield

home, as I walked back to our house, that I developed the theory of the black hole, and it helped me immeasurably in conducting this business of steering drunks around the Point. The idea was this — that at a certain age, a black hole emerged in the middle of your life, and everything got sucked into it, and you knew, forever afterward, that it was there, this dense negative space, and yet you went on, you struggled, you made your money, you had some babies, you got wasted, and you pretended it wasn't there and never looked directly at it, if you could manage the trick. I imagined that this black hole existed somewhere just behind you and also somewhere just in front of you, so that you were always leaving it behind and entering it at the same time. I hadn't worked out the spatial thing too carefully, but that's what I imagined. Sometimes the hole was only a pinprick in the mind, often it was vast, frequently it fluctuated, beating like a heart, but it was always there, and when you got drunk, thinking to escape, you only noticed it more. Anyway, when I discovered this, much like an astronomer gazing out at the universe, I thought I had the key — and it became a policy with me never to let one of my drunks think too much and fall backward or forward into the black hole. We're going home, I would say to them — we're just going home.

I wondered how old Mrs. Gurney was, and guessed thirty-seven. I imagined her black hole was about the size of a sewer cap.

Mrs. Gurney sat down on the hull of an overturned life raft. She reached up under her skirt and pulled her nylons off, rolling them down her legs, tossing the little black doughnuts into the wind. I fetched them, too, and stuffed them into the straps of her sandals.

"Much better," she said.

"We're not far now, Mrs. Gurney. We'll have you home in no time."

She managed to stand up on her own. She floated past me, heading toward the sea. A tangle of ghostly gray driftwood — old tree stumps, logs loosed from booms, planks — barred the way, being too treacherous for her to climb in such a drunken state, I thought, but Mrs. Gurney just kept going, her hair exploding in the wind, her skirt billowing like a sail, her arms wavering like a trapeze artist's high up on the wire.

"Mrs. Gurney?" I called.

"I want —," she started, but the wind tore her words away. Then she sat down on a log, and when I got there, she was holding her head in her hands and vomiting between her legs. Vomit, and the spectacle of adults vomiting, was one of the unpleasant aspects of this job. I hated to see these people in such an abject position. Still, after three years, I knew in which closets the mops and sponges and cleansers were kept in quite a few houses on the Point.

I patted Mrs. Gurney's shoulder, and said, "That's okay, that's okay, just go right ahead. You'll feel much better when it's all out."

She choked and spat, and a trail of silver hung from her lip down to the sand. "Oh, damn it all, Kurt. Just damn it all to hell." She raised her head. "Look at me, just look at me, will you?"

She looked a little wretched, but all right. I'd seen worse.

"Have a cigarette, Mrs. Gurney," I said. "Calm down."

I didn't smoke, myself — thinking it was a disgusting habit — but I'd observed from past experience that a cigarette must taste good to a person who has just thrown up. A cigarette or two seemed to calm people right down, giving them something simple to concentrate on.

Mrs. Gurney handed me her cigarettes. I shook one from the pack and stuck it in my mouth. I struck half a dozen matches before I got one going, cupping the flame against the wind in the style of old war movies. I puffed the smoke. I passed Mrs. Gurney the cigarette, and she dragged on it, abstracted, gazing off. I waited, and let her smoke in peace.

"I feel god-awful," Mrs. Gurney groaned.

"It'll go away, Mrs. Gurney. You're drunk. We just have to get you home."

"Look at my skirt," she said.

True, she'd messed it up a little, barfing on herself, but it was nothing a little soap and water couldn't fix. I told her that.

"How old am I, Kurt?" she retorted.

I pretended to think it over, then aimed low.

"Twenty-nine? Good God!" Mrs. Gurney stared out across the water, at the deep, black shadow of Hat Island, and I looked, too, and it was remarkable, the way that darkness carved itself out of the darkness all around. But I could marvel over this when I was off duty.

"I'm thirty-eight, Kurt," she screamed. "Thirty-eight, thirty-eight, thirty-eight!"

I was losing her. She was heading for ten on a scale of ten.

"On a dark night, bumping around," she said, "you can't tell the difference between thirty-eight and forty. Fifty! Sixty!" She pitched her cigarette in a high, looping arc that exploded against a log in a spray of gold sparks. "Where am I going, God damn it?"

"You're going home, Mrs. Gurney. Hang tough."

"I want to die."

A few boats rocked in the wind, and a seal moaned out on the diving raft, the cries carrying away from us, south, downwind. A red warning beacon flashed out on the sandbar. Mrs. Gurney clambered over the driftwood and weaved across the wet sand toward the sea. She stood by the shoreline, and for a moment I thought she might hurl herself into the breach, but she didn't. She stood on the shore's edge, the white waves swirling at her feet, and dropped her skirt around her ankles. She was wearing a silky white slip underneath, the sheen like a bike reflector in the moonlight. She waded out into the water and squatted down, scrubbing her skirt. Then she walked out of the water and stretched herself on the sand.

"Mrs. Gurney?"

"I've got the fucking spins."

Her eyes were closed. I suggested that she open them. "It makes a difference," I said. "And sit up, Mrs. Gurney. That makes a difference, too."

"You've had the spins?" Mrs. Gurney asked. "Don't tell me you sneak into your mother's liquor cabinet, Kurt

Pittman. Don't tell me that. Please, just please spare me that. Jesus Christ, I couldn't take it. Really, I couldn't take it, Kurt. Just shut the fuck up about that, all right?"

I'd never taken a drink in my life. "I don't drink, Mrs. Gurney."

"I don't drink, Mrs. Gurney," she repeated. "You prig."

I wondered what time it was, and how long we'd been gone.

"Do you know how suddenly life can turn?" Mrs. Gurney asked. "How bad it can get?"

At first I didn't say anything. This kind of conversation didn't lead anywhere. Mrs. Gurney was drunk and belligerent. She was looking for an enemy. "We need to get you home, Mrs. Gurney," I said. "That's my only concern."

"Your only concern," Mrs. Gurney said, imitating me again. "Lucky you."

I stood there, slightly behind Mrs. Gurney. I was getting tired, but sitting down in the sand might indicate to her that where we were was okay, and it wasn't. We needed to get beyond this stage, this tricky stage of groveling in the sand and feeling depressed, and go to sleep.

"We're not getting anywhere like this," I said.

"I've got cottonmouth," Mrs. Gurney said. She made fish movements with her mouth. She was shivering, too. She clasped her knees and tucked her head between her legs, trying to ball herself up like a potato bug.

"Kurt," Mrs. Gurney said, looking up at me, "do you think I'm beautiful?"

I switched the sandals I was holding to the other hand.

First I'll tell you what I said, and then I'll tell you what I was thinking. I said yes, and I said it immediately. And why? Because I sensed that questions that didn't receive an immediate response fell away into silence and were never answered. They got sucked into the black hole. I'd observed this, and I knew the trick was to close the gap in Mrs. Gurney's mind, to bridge that spooky silence between the question and the answer. There she was, drunk, sick, shivering, loveless, sitting in the sand and asking me, a mere boy, if I thought she was beautiful. I said yes, because I knew it wouldn't hurt, or cost me anything but one measly breath, though that wasn't really my answer. The answer was in the immediacy, the swiftness of my response, stripped of all uncertainty and hesitation.

"Yes," I said.

Mrs. Gurney lay down again in the sand. She unbuttoned her blouse and unfastened her brassiere.

I scanned the dark, and fixed my eyes on a tug hauling a barge north through the Passage, up to the San Juans.

Mrs. Gurney sat up. She shrugged out of her blouse and slipped her bra off and threw them into the wind. Again, I fetched her things from where they fell, and held the bundle at my side, waiting.

"That's better," Mrs. Gurney said, arching her back and stretching her hands in the air, waggling them as if she were some kind of dignitary in a parade. "The wind blowing, it's like a spirit washing over you."

"We should go, Mrs. Gurney."

"Sit, Kurt, sit," she said, patting the wet sand. The

imprint of her hand remained there a few seconds, then flattened and vanished. The tide was coming in fast, and it would be high tonight, with the moon full.

I crouched down, a few feet away.

"So you think I'm beautiful?" Mrs. Gurney said. She stared ahead, not looking at me, letting the words drift in the wind.

"This really isn't a question of beauty or not beauty, Mrs. Gurney."

"No?"

"No," I said. "I know your husband doesn't love you, Mrs. Gurney. That's the problem here."

"Beauty," she sang.

"No. Like they say, beauty is in the eye of the beholder. You don't have a beholder anymore, Mrs. Gurney."

"The moon and the stars," she said, "the wind and the sea."

Wind, sea, stars, moon: we were in uncharted territory, and it was my fault. I'd let us stray from the goal, and now it was nowhere in sight. I had to steer this thing back on course, or we'd end up talking about God.

"Get dressed, Mrs. Gurney; it's cold. This isn't good. We're going home."

She clasped her knees, and rocked back and forth. She moaned. "It's so far."

"It's not far," I said. "We can see it from here."

"Someday I'm leaving all this to you," Mrs. Gurney said, waving her hands around in circles, pointing at just about everything in the world. "When I get it from my husband, after the divorce, I'm leaving it to you. That's a promise, Kurt. I mean that. It'll be in my will. You'll get a call. You'll get a call and you'll know I'm dead. But you'll be happy, you'll be very happy, because all of this will belong to you."

Her house was only a hundred yards away. A wind sock, full of the air that passed through it, whipped back and forth on a tall white pole. Her two kids had been staying in town most of that summer. I wasn't sure if they were up this weekend. She'd left the porch light on for herself.

"You'd like all this, right?" Mrs. Gurney asked.

"Now is not the time to discuss it," I said.

Mrs. Gurney lay back down in the sand. "The stars have tails," she said. "When they spin."

I looked up; they seemed fixed in place to me.

"The first time I fell in love I was fourteen. I fell in love when I was fifteen, I fell in love when I was sixteen, seventeen, eighteen. I just kept falling, over and over," Mrs. Gurney said. "This eventually led to marriage." She packed a lump of wet sand on her chest. "It's so stupid — you know where I met him?"

I assumed she was referring to Jack, to Mr. Gurney. "No," I said.

"On a golf course, can you believe it?"

"Do you golf, Mrs. Gurney?"

"No! Hell no."

"Does Jack?"

"No."

I couldn't help her — it's the stories that don't make sense that drunks like to repeat. From some people, I'd been hearing the same stories every summer for the last three years — the kind everyone thinks is special, never realizing how everyone tells pretty much the same one, never realizing how all those stories blend, one to the next, and bleed into each other.

"I'm thirsty," Mrs. Gurney said. "I'm so homesick."

"We're close now," I said.

"That's not what I mean," she said. "You don't know what I mean."

"Maybe not," I said. "Please put your shirt on, Mrs. Gurney."

"I'll kill myself," Mrs. Gurney said. "I'll go home and I'll kill myself."

"That won't get you anywhere."

"It'll show them."

"You'd just be dead, Mrs. Gurney. Then you'd be forgotten."

"Crutchfield isn't forgotten. Poor Crutchfield. The flag's at half-mast."

"This year," I said. "Next year it'll be back where it always is."

"My boys wouldn't forget."

That was certainly true, I thought, but I didn't want to get into it.

Mrs. Gurney sat up. She shook her head back and forth, wildly, and sand flew from it. Then she stood, wobbling. I held the shirt out to her, looking down. She wiggled her toes, burrowing them into the sand.

"Look at me," Mrs. Gurney said.

"I'd rather not, Mrs. Gurney," I said. "Tomorrow you'll be glad I didn't."

For a moment we didn't speak, and into that empty

space rushed the wind, the waves, the moaning seal out on the diving raft. I looked up, into Mrs. Gurney's eyes, which were dark green, and floating in tears. She stared back, but kind of vaguely, and I wondered what she saw.

I had the feeling that the first to flinch would lose.

She took the shirt from my hand.

I looked.

In this, I had no experience, but I knew what I saw was not young flesh. Her breasts sagged away like sacks of wet sand, slumping off to either side. They were quite enormous, I thought, although I had nothing to compare them with. There were long whitish scars on them, as if a wild man or a bear had clawed her. The nipples were purple in the moonlight, and they puckered in the cold wind. The gold, squiggling loops of chain shone against the dark of her neck, and the V of her tan line made everything else seem astonishingly white. The tan skin of her chest looked like parchment, like the yellowed, crinkled page of some ancient text, maybe the Bible, or the Constitution, the original copy, or even the rough draft.

Mrs. Gurney slipped the shirt over her shoulders and let it flap there in the wind. It blew off and tumbled down the beach. She sighed. Then she stepped closer and leaned toward me. I could smell her — the pepper, the bananas.

"Mrs. Gurney," I said, "let's go home now." The tide was high enough for us to feel the first foamy white reaches of the waves wash around our feet. The receding waves dragged her shirt into the sea, and then the incoming waves flung it back. It hung there in the margin, agitated. We were looking into each other's eyes. Up so close, there was nothing familiar in hers; they were just glassy and dark and expressionless.

It was then, I was sure, that her hand brushed the front of my trunks. I don't remember too much of what I was thinking, if I was, and this, this not thinking too clearly, might have been my downfall. What is it out there that indicates the right way? I might have gone down all the way. I might have sunk right there. I knew all the words for it, and they were all short and brutal. Fuck, poke, screw. A voice told me I could get away with it. Who will know the difference? the voice asked. It said, Go for it. And I knew the voice, knew it was the same voice that told Mr. Crutchfield to go ahead, fuck around. We were alone — nothing out there but the moon and the sea. I looked at Mrs. Gurney, looked into her eyes, and saw two black lines pouring out of them and running in crazy patterns down her cheeks.

I felt I should be gallant, or tender, and kiss Mrs. Gurney. I felt I should say something, then I felt I should be quiet. It seemed as if the moment were poised, as if everything were fragile, and held together with silence.

We moved up the beach, away from the shore and the incoming tide, and the sand beneath the surface still held some of the day's warmth.

I took off my T-shirt. "Put this on," I said.

She tugged it on, inside out, and I gathered up her sandals and stockings and her bra. We kept silent. We worked our way over the sand, over the tangle of driftwood, the wind heaving at us from the north.

We crossed the boardwalk, and I held Mrs. Gurney's

elbow as we went up the steps of her house. Inside, I found the aspirin and poured a glass of apple cider, and brought these to her in bed, where she'd already curled up beneath a heavy Mexican blanket. She looked like she was sleeping underneath a rug. "I'm thirsty," she said, and drank down the aspirin with the juice. A lamp was on. Mrs. Gurney's silver hair splayed out against the pillow, poking like bike spokes, every which way. I knelt beside the bed, and she touched my hand and parted her lips to speak, but I squeezed her hand and her eyes closed. Soon she was asleep.

As I was going downstairs, her two boys, Mark and Timmy, came out of their bedroom, and stared at me from the landing.

"Mommy home?" asked Timmy, who was three.

"Yeah," I said. "She's in bed, she's sleeping."

They stood there on the lighted landing, blinking and rubbing knuckles in their eyes, and I stood below them on the steps in the dark.

"Where's the sitter?" I asked.

"She fell asleep," Timmy said.

"You guys should be asleep, too."

"I can't sleep," Timmy said. "Tell a bedtime story."

"I don't know any bedtime stories," I said.

Back home, inside our house, the bright light and smoke stung my eyes. The living room was crowded, but I knew everybody — the Potters, the Shanks, the Capstands, etc. It was noisy and shrill, and someone had cranked up the Victrola, and one of my grandfather's old records was sending a sea of hissing static through the room. I could see on the mantel, through the curling smoke, the shrine Mother had made for Father: his Silver Star and Purple Heart, which he got in Lao Bao, up near Khe Sanh, near the DMZ when he was a medic. His diploma from medical school angled cockeyed off a cut nail. A foul ball he'd caught at a baseball game, his reading glasses, a pocketknife, a stethoscope, a framed Hippocratic oath with snakes wreathed around what looked like a barber pole. I saw Mother flit through the kitchen with a silver cocktail shaker, jerking it like a percussion instrument. She just kept pacing like a caged animal, rattling cracked ice in the shaker. I couldn't hear any distinct voices above the party noise. I stood there awhile. No one seemed to notice me until Fred, three sheets to the wind, as they say, hoisted his empty glass in the air, and said, "Hey, Captain!"

I went into the kitchen. Mother set down the shaker and looked at me. I gave her a hug. "I'm back," I said.

Then I crossed into my room and stripped the sheets from my bed. I hung them out the window and shook the sand away. I tossed the sheets back on the bed and stretched out, but I couldn't get to sleep. I got up and pulled one of Father's old letters out from under my mattress. I went out the back door. It was one of those nights on the Point when the blowing wind, the waves breaking in crushed white lines against the shore, the grinding sand, the moonwashed silhouettes of the huddled houses, the slapping of buoys offshore — when all of this seems to have been going on for a long, long time, and you feel eternity looking down on you. I sat on the swing. The letter was torn at the creases, and I opened it carefully, tilting it into the moonlight. It was dated 1966, and written to Mother. The print was smudged and hard to see.

First, the old news: thank you for the necktie. I'm not sure when I'll get a chance to wear it, but thanks. Now for my news. I've been wounded, but don't worry. I'm OK.

For several days a company had been deployed on the perimeter of this village — the rumor was that somehow the fields had been planted with VC mines. The men work with tanks — picture tanks moving back and forth over a field like huge lawnmowers. They clear the way by exploding the mines. Generally VC mines are anti-personnel, and the idea is that the tanks are supposed to set off the mines and absorb the explosions. Tanks can easily sustain the blows, and the men inside are safe. A textbook operation. Simple. Yesterday they set off twelve mines. Who knows how they got there?

Clearing the perimeter took several days. Last night they thought they were done. But as the men were jumping off the tanks, one of them landed right on a mine. I was the first medic to reach him. His feet and legs were blown off, blown away up to his groin. I've never seen anything so terrible, but here's what I remember most clearly: a piece of shrapnel had penetrated his can of shaving cream, and it was shooting a stream of white foam about five feet in the air. Blood spilling everywhere, and then this fountain of white arcing out of his back. The pressure inside the can kept hissing. The kid was maybe nineteen. "Doc, I'm a mess," he said. I called in a medevac. I started packing dressings, then saw his eyes lock up, and tried to revive him with heart massage. The kid died before the shaving cream was done spraying.

Everything became weirdly quiet, considering the havoc, and then suddenly the LZ got hot and we took fire — fifteen minutes of artillery and incoming mortar fire, then quiet again. Nothing, absolutely nothing. I took a piece of shrapnel in my back, but don't worry. I'm all right, though I won't have occasion to wear that tie soon. I didn't even know I was wounded until I felt the blood, and even then I thought it was someone else's.

Strange, during that fifteen minutes of action I felt no fear. But there's usually not much contact with the enemy. Often you don't see a single VC the whole time. Days pass without any contact. They're out there, you know, yet you never see them. Just mines, booby traps. I'm only a medic, and my contact with the enemy is rarely direct — what I see are the wounded men and the dead, the bodies. I see the destruction, and I have begun to both fear and hate the Vietnamese — even here in South Vietnam, I can't tell whose side they're on. Every day I visit a nearby village and help a local doctor vaccinate children. The morning after the attack I felt the people in the village were laughing at me because they knew an American had died. Yesterday I returned to the same village. Everything quiet, business as usual, but I stood there, surrounded by hooches, thinking of that dead kid, and for a moment I felt the urge to even the score somehow.

What am I saying, sweetie? I'm a medic, trained to save lives. Every day I'm closer to death than most people ever get, except in their final second on earth. It's a world of hurt — that's the phrase we use — and things happen over here, things you just can't keep to yourself. I've seen what happens to men who try. They're consumed by what they've seen and done, they grow obsessive, and slowly they lose sight of the job they're supposed to be doing. I have no hard proof of this, but I think in this condition men open themselves up to attack. You've got to talk things out, get everything very clear in your mind. Lucky for me I've got a buddy over here who's been under fire too, and can understand what I'm feeling. That helps.

I'm sorry to write like this, but in your letter you said you wanted to know everything. It's not in my power to say what this war means to you or anyone back home, but I can describe what happens, and if you want, I'll continue doing that. For me, at least, it's a comfort to know someone's out there, far away, who can't really understand, and I hope is never able to. I'll write again soon.

All love,
Henry

·

I'd snagged this letter from a box Mother kept in her room, under the bed. There were other kinds of letters in the box, letters about love and family and work, but I didn't think Mother would miss this one, which was just about war. Father never talked much about his tours in Vietnam, but he would if I asked. Out of respect, I learned not to ask too much, but I knew about Zippo raids, trip flares, bouncing bettys, hand frags, satchel charges, and such, and when he was angry, or sad, Father often peppered his speech with slang he'd picked up, like *titi*, which means "little," and *didi mow*, which means "go quickly," and *xin loi*, meaning "sorry about that."

I tucked the letter away. I got the swing going real good, and I rose up, then fell, rose and fell, seeing, then not seeing. When the swing was going high enough I let go, and sailed through the open air, landing in an explosion of soft sand. I wiped the grains out of my eyes. My eyes watered, and everything was unclear. Things toppled and blew in the wind. A striped beach umbrella rolled across the playfield, twirling like a pinwheel. A sheet from someone's clothesline flapped loose and sailed away. I thought of my nightmare, of Father's balloon tied to a stringbean. I looked up at the sky, and it was black, with some light. There were stars, millions of them like tiny holes in something, and the moon, like a bigger hole in the same thing. White holes. I thought of Mrs. Gurney and her blank eyes and the black pouring out of them. Was it the wind, a sudden gust kicking up and brushing my trunks? It happened so quickly. Had she tried to touch me? Had she? I stretched out in the sand. The wind gave me goose bumps.

Shivering, I listened. From inside the house, I heard the men laughing, the ice clinking, the women shrieking. Everything in there was still hysterical. I'd never get to sleep. I decided to stay awake. They would all be going home, but until then I'd wait outside.

I lay there, very quietly. I brushed some sand off me. I waited.

It was me who found Father, that morning. I'd gone up to get some creosote out of the trunk of his car. It was a cold, gray, misty morning, the usual kind we have, and in the grass field above the parking lot there was a family of deer, chewing away, looking around, all innocent. And there he was, sitting in the car. I opened the passenger door. At first my eyes kind of separated from my brain, and I saw everything, real slow, like you might see a movie, or something far away that wasn't happening to you. Some of his face was gone. One of his eyes was staring out. He was still breathing, but his lungs worked like he'd swallowed a yard of chunk gravel or sand. He was twitching. I touched his hand and the fingers curled around mine, gripping, but it was just nerves, an old reaction or something, because he was brain-dead already. My imagination jumped right out of its box when he grabbed me. I knew right away I was being grabbed by a dead man. I got away. I ran away. In our house I tried to speak, but there were no words. I started pounding the walls and kicking over the furniture and breaking stuff. I couldn't see, I heard falling. I ran around the house holding and ripping at my head. Eventually Mother caught me. I just pointed up to the car. You understand, I miss Father, miss having him around to tell me what's right and what's wrong, or to talk about *boom-boom,* which is sex, or just to go salmon fishing out by Hat Island, and not worry about things, either way, but I also have to say, never again do I want to see anything like what I saw that morning. I never, as long as I live, want to find another dead person. He wasn't even a person then, just a blown-up thing, just crushed-up garbage. Part of his head was blasted away, and there was blood and hair and bone splattered on the windshield. It looked like he'd just driven the car through something awful, like he needed to use the windshield wipers, needed to switch the blades on high and clear the way, except that the wipers wouldn't do him any good, because the mess was all on the inside.

HER REAL NAME

---

for P.L.A.

I

THE GIRL'S SCALP looked as though it had been singed by fire — strands of thatchy red hair snaked away from her face, then settled against her skin, pasted there by sweat and sunscreen and the blown grit and dust of travel. For a while her thin hair had remained as light and clean as the down of a newborn chick, but it was getting hotter as they drove west, heading into a summer-long drought that scorched the landscape, that withered the grass and melted the black tar between expansion joints in the road and bloated like balloons the bodies of raccoon and deer and dog and made everything on the highway ahead ripple like a mirage through waves of rising heat. Since leaving Fargo, it had been too hot to wear the wig, and it now lay on the seat between them, still holding within its webbing the shape of her head. Next to it, a bag of orange candy — *smiles,* she called them — spilled across the vinyl. Sugar crystals ran into the dirty stitching and stuck to her thigh. Gum wrappers and greasy white bags littered the floor, and on the dash, amid a flotsam of plastic cups, pennies, and matchbooks, a bumper sticker curled in the heat. EXPECT A MIRACLE, it read.

The girl cradled a black Bible in her lap, the leather covers as worn and ragged as old tennis shoes. The inner leaf contained a family tree dating back to 1827, names tightly scrawled in black against yellowing parchment, a genealogy as ponderous as those kept in Genesis, the book of the generations of Adam. The list of ancestors on the inner leaf was meaningless ancient history to the man, whose name was Jones, but the girl said her family had carried that same Bible with them wherever they went, for one hundred and fifty years, and that she wanted it with her too. "That's me," the girl had said, showing Jones her name, the newest of all, penned in generous loops of Bic blue. She'd written it in herself along the margin of the page. *b. 1960–*. The girl read different passages aloud as they drove, invoking a mix of epic beauty and bad memories, of Exodus and the leather belt her stepfather used to beat her when she broke a commandment — one of the original ten or one of his additions. Jones wasn't sure what faith she placed in the austere Christianity of her forefathers, but reading aloud seemed to cast a spell over her. She had a beautiful church-trained voice that lifted each verse into a soothing melody, a song whose tune of succor rose and fell somewhere beyond the harsh demands of faith. Only minutes before she'd read herself to sleep with a passage from Jeremiah.

Now, as if she felt Jones staring, the girl stirred.

"You were looking at me," she said. "You were thinking something."

Her face was shapeless, soft and pale as warm putty.

"I could feel it," she said. "Where are we?"

They hadn't gone more than a mile since she'd dozed off. She reached for the candy on the seat.

"You hungry? You want a smile, Jones?"

"No, none for me," Jones said.

"A Life Saver?" She held the unraveled package out.

"Nothing, thanks."

"Me eating candy, and my teeth falling out." The girl licked the sugar off a smile and asked, "How far to Las Vegas?"

Jones jammed a tape in the eight-track. He was driving a 1967 Belvedere he'd bought for seven hundred dollars cash in Newport News, and it had come with a bulky eight-track, like an atavistic organ, bolted beneath the glove box. He'd found two tapes in the trunk, and now, after fifteen thousand miles, he was fairly sick of both Tom Jones and Steppenwolf. But he preferred the low-fidelity noise of either tape to the sound of himself lying.

"Why don't you come with me, little girl," he sang along, in a high, mocking falsetto, "on a magic carpet ride."

"How far?" the girl asked.

Jones adjusted his grip on the steering wheel. "Another day, maybe."

She seemed to fall asleep again, her dry-lidded eyes shut like a lizard's, her parched, flaking lips parted, her frail body given over to the car's gentle rocking. Jones turned his attention back to the road, a hypnotic black line snaking through waves of yellow grass. It seemed to Jones that they'd been traveling through eastern Montana forever, that the same two or three trees, the same two or three farmhouses and grain silos were rushing past like scenery in an old movie, only suggesting movement. Endless fields, afire in the bright sun, were occasionally broken by stands of dark cottonwood or the gutted chassis of a rusting car. Collapsing barns leaned over in the grass, giving in to the hot wind and the insistent flatness, as if passively accepting the laws of a world whose only landmark, as far as Jones could see, was the level horizon.

"He's out there," the girl said. "I can feel him out there when I close my eyes. He knows where we are."

"I doubt that very much," Jones said.

The girl struggled to turn, gripping the headrest. She looked through the rear window at the warp of the road as it narrowed to a pinprick on the pale edge of the world they'd left behind: it was out of the vanishing point that her father would come.

"I expect he'll be caught up soon," she said. "He's got a sense. One time he predicted an earthquake."

"It's a big country," Jones said. "We could've gone a million other ways. Maybe if you think real hard about Florida that'll foul up his super-duper predicting equipment."

"Prayer," the girl said. "He prays. Nothing fancy. We're like Jonah sneaking on that boat in Tarshish; they found him out."

The girl closed her eyes; she splashed water on her face and chest.

"It's so hot," she said. "Tell me some more about the Eskimos."

"I'm running out of things to say about Eskimos,"
Jones said. "I only read that one book."

"Say old stuff, I don't care."

He searched his memory for what he remembered of
Knud Rasmussen.

"Nothing's wasted," Jones said. "They use everything. The Inuit can make a sled out of a slain dog. They
kill the dog and skin it, then cut the hide into two strips."

"I'm burning alive," the girl said.

"They roll up the hide and freeze the strips in water
to make the runners. Then they join the runners together
with the dog's rib bones." Jones nibbled the corner of an
orange smile. "One minute the dog's pulling the sled, the
next minute he is the sled." He saw that the girl was
asleep. "That's irony," he said and then repeated the word.
"Irony." It sounded weak, inadequate; it described nothing; he drove silently on. Out through the windshield he
saw a landscape too wide for the eye to measure — the
crushing breadth of the burnt fields and the thin black
thread of road vanishing into a vast blue sky as if the clouds
massed on the horizon were distant cities, and they were
going to them.

She'd been working the pumps and the register at a cross-
roads station in southern Illinois, a rail-thin girl with stiff
red hair the color of rust, worried, chipped nails, and green
eyes without luster. She wore gray coveralls that ballooned
over her body like a clown's outfit, the long legs and sleeves
rolled into thick cuffs. "I've never seen the ocean," she'd
said, pointing to the remains of a peeling bumper sticker

on Jones's car. . . . BE SAILING, it read. She stood on the pump island while Jones filled his tank. The hooded blue lights above them pulsed in sync to the hovering sound of cicadas, and both were a comforting close presence in the black land spreading out around the station. Jones wanted to tell the girl to look around her, right now: this flat patch of nothing was as good as an ocean. Instead, making conversation, Jones said, "I just got out of the navy."

"You from around here?" she asked.

"Nope," Jones said.

He topped off his tank and reached into the car where he kept his money clipped to the sun visor.

"I knew that," she said. "I seen your plates."

Jones handed her a twenty from his roll of muster pay. The money represented for him his final six months in the navy, half a year in which he hadn't once set foot on land. Tired of the sea, knowing he'd never make a career out of it, on his last tour Jones had refused the temptations of shore leave, hoping to hit land with enough of a stake to last him a year. Now, as he looked at the dwindling roll, he was torn between exhaustion and a renewed desire to move on before he went broke.

"Where in Virginia you from?"

"I'm not," Jones said. "I bought the car in Newport News. Those are just old plates."

"That's too bad," the girl said. "I like the name. Virginia. Don't you?"

"I guess it's not special to me one way or the other," Jones said.

The girl folded the twenty in half and ran her thin

fingers back and forth over the crease. That she worked in a gas station in the middle of nowhere struck Jones as sexy, and now he looked at her closely, trying to decide whether or not he wanted to stop a night or two in Carbondale. Except for the strange texture and tint of her red hair, he thought she looked good, and the huge coveralls, rippling in the breeze, made her seem sweet and lost, somehow innocent and alone in a way that gave Jones the sudden confidence that he could pick her up without much trouble.

"You gonna break that?" Jones asked, nodding at the bill.

Her arm vanished entirely as she reached into the deep pocket of her coveralls and pulled out a roll of bills stained black with grease and oil. Jones took the change, then looked off, around the station. In the east a dome of light rose above Carbondale, a pale yellow pressing out against the night sky. The road running in front of the station was empty except for a spotlight that shone on a green dinosaur and a Sinclair sign that spun on a pole above it.

"Don't get scared, working out here?" he asked.

"Nah," she said. "Hardly anyone comes out this way, 'less they're like you, 'less they're going somewhere. Had a man from Vernal gas here the other night. That's in Utah."

"Still —"

"Some nights I wouldn't care if I got robbed."

Jones took his toilet kit — a plastic sack that contained a thin, curved bonelike bar of soap, a dull razor, and a balding toothbrush — out of the glove box. "You mind if I wash up?"

"Washroom's around back," she said. "By the propane tanks."

In the bathroom, he took off his T-shirt and washed himself with a wetted towel, watching his reflection in the mirror above the sink as though it were someone else, someone from his past. Gray eyes, a sharp sculpted jaw, ears that jutted absurdly from his close-cropped head: a navy face. Six months of shipboard isolation had left him with little sense of himself outside of his duties as an officer. In that time, held in the chrysalis of his berth, he'd forgotten not only what he looked like, but what other people might see when they looked at him. Now he was a civilian. He decided to shave, lathering up with the bar of soap. The mustache came off in four or five painful strokes.

For a moment the warm breeze was bracing against his cleanly shaven face. He stood in the lot, a little stiff, at attention, and when the girl waved to him from the cashier's window, Jones saluted.

"See you later," he said.

"Okay," she said.

Jones drove away, stopping at a convenience store about a mile down the road. He grabbed two six-packs, a cheap Styrofoam cooler, and a bag of ice and wandered down the aisle where the toys were kept. He selected a pink gun that fired rubber suction darts. He returned to the station and parked his car in the shadow of the dinosaur. He waited. The girl sat in the glass booth behind a rack of road atlases, suddenly the sweetheart of every town

he'd traveled through in the last few months. To be with
someone who knew his name, to hear another voice would
be enough for tonight. Jones twisted open a beer and loaded
the dart gun. He licked the suction tip, took aim and fired.

"Hey," the girl shouted.

"Wanna go somewhere?" Jones asked.

They'd crossed the Mississippi three weeks ago and driven
north through Iowa, staying in motels and eating in res-
taurants, enjoying high times until his money began to run
out. Then they started sleeping in the car, parked at rest
stops or in empty lots, arms and legs braided together in
the backseat of the Belvedere. One morning Jones had gone
to a bakeshop and bought a loaf of day-old sourdough bread
for thirty-five cents. It was the cool blue hour before dawn,
but already, as he crossed the parking lot, the sky was
growing pale, and the patches of tar were softening beneath
his shoes, and in the sultry air the last weak light of the
street lamps threw off dull coronas of yellow and pink.
Only one other car was parked in the empty lot, and its
windows had been smashed out, a spray of glass scattered
like seeds across the asphalt. As Jones approached the
Belvedere, he saw the girl slowly lift the hair away from
her head. It was as if he were witness to some miracle of
revelation set in reverse, as if the rising sun and the new
day had not bestowed but instead stripped the world of
vision, exposed and left it bare. Her skull was blue, a
hidden thing not meant for the light. Jones opened her
door. She held the wig of curly red hair in her lap.

"Damn," he said. He paced off a small circle in the
parking lot.

The girl combed her fingers calmly through the hair on her lap. She'd understood when she removed the wig that revealing herself to Jones would tip fate irrevocably. She felt that in this moment she would know Jones and know him forever. She waited for Jones to spend his shock and anger, afraid that when he cooled down she might be on her way back to Carbondale, to the gas station and her stepfather and the church and the prayers for miraculous intercession. When Jones asked what was wrong with her, and she told him, he punted the loaf of sourdough across the empty lot.

"Why haven't you said anything?"

"What was I supposed to say, Jones?"

"The truth might've made a good start."

"Seems to me you've been having yourself a fine time without it," she said. "Hasn't been all that crucial so far."

"Jesus Christ."

"Besides, I wouldn't be here now if I'd told you. You'd have been long gone."

Jones denied it. "You don't know me from Adam," he said.

"Maybe not," she said. She set the wig on her head. "I'll keep it on if you think I'm ugly." The girl swung her legs out of the car and walked across the lot. She picked up the bread and brought it back. "These things drag out," she said.

She brushed pebbles and dirt and splinters of glass from the crust and then cracked the loaf in half.

"You didn't get any orange juice, did you?" she asked. "This old bread needs orange juice."

She reached inside and tore a hunk of clean white

bread from the core and passed the loaf to Jones. He ate a piece and calmed down.

"Who knows how long I've got?" she said.

When they headed out again that morning, going west seemed inevitable — driving into the sun was too much to bear, and having it at their backs in the quiet and vacant dawn gave them the feeling, however brief, that they could outrace it. It was 1977, it was August, it was the season when the rolling fields were feverish with sunflowers turning on withered stalks to reach the light, facing them in the east as they drove off at dawn, gazing after them in the west as the sun set and they searched the highway ahead for the softly glowing neon strip, for the revolving signs and lighted windows and the melancholy trickle of small-town traffic that would bloom brightly on the horizon and mean food and a place to stop for the night. If Jones wasn't too tired, he pushed on, preferring the solitude of night driving, when actual distances collapsed unseen, and the car seemed to float unmoored through limitless space, the reassuring hum of tires rolling beneath him, the lights of towns hovering across the darkened land like constellations in a warm universe. By day, he stopped only when the girl wanted to see a natural wonder, a landmark, a point of historical interest. Early this morning they'd visited the valley of the Little Bighorn. Silence held sway over the sight, a silence that touched the history of a century ago and then reached beyond it, running back to the burnt ridges and bluffs and to a time when the flat golden plain in the West had not yet felt the weight of footprints. Jones watched the girl search among the huddled white markers, looking for the blackened stone where Custer fell. She'd climbed over the wrought-iron fence to stand beside the stone, and a bull snake cooling in the shadow slithered off through the yellow grass. She seemed okay, not really sick, only a little odd and alien when she took off the wig. Now and then Jones would look at the girl and think, *You're dying,* but the unvarying heat hammered the days into a dull sameness, and driving induced a kind of amnesia, and for the most part Jones had shoved the idea out of his mind until this morning when they'd discussed their next move.

"We could drive to Nevada," she'd said. "Seems we're headed that direction, anyhow."

"Maybe," Jones had said.

"It only takes an hour to get married," the girl said, "and they rent you the works. A veil, flowers. We'll gamble. I've never done that. Have you? Roulette — what do you think, Jones?"

"I said maybe."

"Jones," she said. "I'm not into maybe."

"I don't know," Jones said. "I haven't thought it out."

"What's to think?" the girl said. "You'd be a widower in no time."

Jones squeezed the girl's knee, knobby and hard like a foal's. "Jesus," he said.

"It's not a big commitment I'm asking for."

"Okay, all right," Jones had said. "Don't get morbid."

Night fell, and the highway rose into the mountains. With the continental divide coming up, Jones couldn't decide whether or not to wake the girl. She didn't like to miss a landmark or border or any attraction advertised on a bill-board. They'd stopped for the Parade of Presidents, America's Heritage in Wax, and to see alligators and prairie dogs and an ostrich and the bleached white bones of dinosaurs, and by now the back of the car was covered with bumper stickers and decals, and the trunk was full of souvenirs she'd bought, snow-filled baubles, bolo ties, beaded Indian belts, engraved bracelets, pennants. Wall Drug, Mount Rushmore, the Little Bighorn, and a bare rutted patch of dirt in the sweet grass that, according to a bullet-riddled placard, was the Lewis and Clark Trail — she'd stocked up on hokey junk and sentimental trinkets, and the stuff now commemorated a wandering path across state lines, over rivers, up mountains, into empty fields where battles had been fought and decided and down the streets of dirty, forgotten towns where once, long ago, something important had happened.

Jones gave her a shake.

"Jones?" She was disoriented, a child spooked on waking in unfamiliar surroundings. "I'm not feeling too good."

"You want to lie down?"

"I could use a beer," the girl said. "Something to kill this."

Jones eased the car over the breakdown line. The mountains cut a crown of darkness out of the night sky, and a row of telephone poles, silhouetted in the starlight, seemed like crosses planted along the highway. He arranged the backseat, shoving his duffle to the floor and unrolling the sleeping bag. The car shook as a semi passed, spraying a phalanx of gravel in its wake.

"Let's get there soon," the girl said.

"Get in back," Jones said.

"I'm praying," she said.

"That's good," he said. Jones ran his hand over the girl's head. Wispy strands of hair pulled loose and stuck to his palm. "We'll stop in the next town."

Back on the road, the wind dried his T-shirt, and the sweat-soaked cotton turned stiff as cardboard. Beneath him the worn tires rolled over the warm asphalt like the murmur of a river. On the move once more, he felt only relief, a sense of his body freed from its strict place in time, drifting through the huddled blue lights of towns named after Indians and cavalrymen and battles, after blind expectations and the comforts of the known past, after the sustaining beliefs and fears of pioneers. Outlook, Savage, Plentywood. Going west, names changed, became deposits of utopian history, places named Hope and Endwell, Wisdom and Independence and Loveland. Whenever the road signs flashed by, luminous for an instant, Jones felt as though he were journeying through a forgotten allegory.

The girl asked, "When do you think we'll be there?"

"We're not going to Las Vegas," Jones said. He had not known his decision until he spoke and heard the words aloud.

"Why not?"

"I'm taking you to a hospital."

"They'll send me home," the girl said.

"They might."

"Dad'll say you abducted me."

"You know that's not the deal."

"Don't matter," the girl said. "He'll say you're working for Satan and his demonic forces, even if you don't know it. He says just about everybody is."

"Well, I'm not," Jones said.

"You might be without you knowing it," the girl said.

They were crossing the Bitterroot. Jones lost radio reception, and so he listened to the girl's prayers, words coming to him in fragments, *Jesus* and *savior* and *amen*, the music of her voice carried away by the wind, choked off whenever she dry-heaved in the seat behind him. Somewhere in western Idaho she fell asleep, and for the next few hours Jones listened to the car tires sing. Outside Spokane, on an illuminated billboard set back in a wheat field, a figure of Jesus walked on water, holding a staff. Jones considered the odd concession to realism: a man walking on water would hardly need to support himself with a crutch. The thought was gone as soon as the billboard vanished behind him. No others took its place. Bored, he searched the radio dial for voices but for long empty stretches pulled in nothing but the sizzle of static, a strange surging cackle filling the car as if suddenly he'd lost contact with earth.

A red neon vacancy sign sputtered ambiguously, the "No" weakly charged and half-lit. Behind the motel and across the railroad tracks, the Columbia River snaked through Wenatchee, flowing wide and quiet, a serene blue vein dividing the town from the apple orchards. The low brown hills were splotched with squares of green, patches of garden carved out of burnt land, and beyond them to the west, rising up, etched into the blue sky, a snowcapped mountain range rimmed the horizon like teeth set in some huge jaw.

"We're here," Jones said.

"Where?"

"Wen-a-tchee," he said.

"Wena-tchee," he tried again.

"Just a place," he said, finally. "Let's get upstairs."

In their room, Jones set the girl on the bed. He spritzed the sheets with tap water, cooling them, and opened the window. A hot breeze pushed the brown burlap curtains into the room. The gray, dusty leaves of an apple tree spread outside the window, and beneath the tree the unnatural blue of a swimming pool shimmered without revealing any depth in the morning sun. A slight breeze rippled the water, and an inflated lifesaver floated aimlessly across the surface.

The girl was kneeling at the foot of the bed, her hands folded and her head bowed in prayer. She was naked; her body a dull, white votary candle, the snuffed flame of her hair a dying red ember.

"Kneel here with me," she said.

"You go ahead," Jones said. He sat on the edge of the bed and pulled off his boots.

"It wouldn't hurt you," she said, "to get on your knees."

"We had this discussion before," he said.

"I believe it was a miracle," the girl said. She was referring to the remission of her cancer, the answered prayers. Her stepfather belonged to an evangelical sect that believed the literal rapture of Judgment Day was near at hand. Several dates he'd predicted for the end of time had already come and gone. Two months ago, he'd taken her out of medical treatment, refusing science in favor of prayer. Her illness bloomed with metaphoric possibilities and large portents for the congregation of the Church of the Redeemer in Carbondale and was used as a kind of augury, variously read as a sign of God's covenant, or as proof of Man's fallenness, his wickedness and sin. For a while she'd been in remission, and news of her cure had brought a host of desperate seekers to the church.

At a display in South Dakota, against the evidence of bones before them, the girl had said dinosaurs didn't die sixty million years ago. "It was about ten thousand years ago," she had insisted. Her stepfather believed they'd been on the boat with Noah.

"Some big-ass boat," Jones had said. Jones no longer had any interest in arguing. But he said, "And now that you're sick again, what's that?"

"It's what the Lord wants."

"There's no talking to you," Jones said.

"We're all just here to bear witness," she said.

"Have your prayers ever been answered?"

"The night you came by the station, I asked for that. I prayed, and you came."

"I was hungry. I wanted a candy bar."

"That's what you think," the girl said. "But you don't know. You don't really know why you stopped, or what the plan is or anything. Who made you hungry? Huh? Think about that."

The rush of words seemed to exhaust her. She

wrapped a corner of the sheet around her finger and re-peated, "Who made you hungry?"

"So you prayed for me, and I came," Jones said. "Me, in particular? Or just someone, anyone?" He stripped off his shirt, wadded it up, and wiped the sweat from his armpits. "Your illness doesn't mean anything. You're just sick, that's all."

Jones cranked the hot water and stayed in the shower, his first in days, until it scalded his skin a splotchy pink. Finished, he toweled off, standing over the girl. She was choking down cries.

"Why don't you take a shower?" Jones said.

"Maybe I should go back home."

"Maybe you should just stand out there on the road and let your old dad's radar find you." Then Jones said, "If that's what you want, I'll get you a bus ticket. You can be on your way tomorrow."

The girl shook her head. "It's noplace to me," she said.

"The Eskimos don't have homes, either," Jones said. "They don't have a word for it. They can't even ask each other, Hey, where do you live?"

I I

Dr. McKillop sat on an apple crate and pulled a flask from his coat pocket. The afternoon heat was bad, but the harsh light was worse; he squinted uphill, vaguely wishing he were sober. It was too late, though, and with a sense of anticipation, of happy fatality, he drank, and the sun-warmed scotch bit hard at the back of his throat. McKillop felt the alcoholic's secret pleasure at submitting to something greater than himself, a realignment with destiny: he took another drink. Swimming in the reflection of the silver flask, he noticed a young white man. He was tall and thin, his cheekbones sharp and high, and in the glare his deep eye sockets seemed empty, pools of cool blue shadow. When the man finally approached, McKillop offered him the flask.

"I was told in town I could find you here," Jones said. McKillop nodded. "You must be desperate."

The doctor wiped dust and sweat from his neck with a sun-bleached bandana. One of the day pickers had fallen from a tree and broken his arm, and McKillop had been called to reset it. He was no longer a doctor, not legally, not since six months ago when he'd been caught prescribing cocaine to himself. The probationary status of his medical license didn't matter to the migrants who worked the apple orchards, and McKillop was glad for the work. It kept trouble at a distance.

"Let me guess," McKillop said. "You don't have any money? Or you're looking for pharmaceuticals?"

"The bartender at Yakima Suzie's gave me your name," Jones said.

"You can get drunk, you can smoke cigars and gamble in a bar. You can find plenty in a bar. I know I have." McKillop pressed a dry brown apple blossom between his fingers, then sniffed beneath his nails. "But a doctor, a doctor you probably shouldn't find in a bar." He looked up at Jones and said, "I've been defrocked."

"I'm not looking for a priest," Jones said. The doctor's stentorian voice and overblown statements were starting to annoy him. The doctor wore huaraches with tire-tread soles, and his toes were caked with dirt, and the long curled nails looked yellow and unhealthy. He knotted his long raggedy hair in a ponytail.

Jones remained silent while a flatbed full of migrants rumbled by, jouncing over a worn two-track of gray dust and chuckholes. The green of the garden, of the orchards he'd seen from the valley, was an illusion; the trail of rising dust blew through the trees and settled and bleached the branches and leaves. A grasshopper spit brown juice on Jones's hand; he flicked it away and said, "I've got a girl in pain."

"Well, a girl in pain." McKillop capped his flask and wiped his neck again. He spat in the dust, a dry glob rolling up thick and hard at his feet. He crushed it away with the rubber heel of his sandal. He looked up into the lattice of leaves, the sun filtered through; many of the apples with a western exposure were still green on the branch. McKillop stood and plucked one of the unripe apples and put it in his pocket. "For later," he said.

The room smelled like rotting mayonnaise. Her body glistened with a yellow liquid. She'd vomited on herself, on the pillows, on the floor. Facedown, she clutched the sheets and tore them from the bed. She rolled over on her back, kicking the mattress and arching herself off the bed, lifting her body, twisting as though she were a wrestler attempting to escape a hold.

Jones pinned her arms against the bed while she bucked, trying to free herself. Her teeth were clenched, then she gasped, gulping for air. Her upper lip held a delicate dew of sweat in a mustache of faint blond hair. She made fists of her thin, skeletal hands, and then opened them, clawing Jones with her yellowed nails.

McKillop drew morphine from a glass vial and found a blue vein running in the girl's arm. A drop of blood beaded where the needle punctured her skin. McKillop dabbed the blood away with the bedsheet and pressed a Band-Aid over the spot.

The girl's body relaxed, as if she were suddenly without skeleton.

Windblown dust clouded the window. Jones slid it open along runners clogged with dirt and desiccated flies and looked down into the motel pool. Lit by underwater lights, it glowed like a jewel. A lawn chair lay on its side near the bottom, gently wavering in an invisible current.

"She needs a doctor," McKillop said.

"That's you," Jones said. "You're the doctor."

McKillop shook his head.

"Don't leave," the girl said. Only her index finger flickered, lifting slightly off the bed, as if all her struggle had been reduced to a tiny spasm.

"Wait outside," Jones said to the doctor.

When he'd gone, Jones turned on the television, a broken color set that bathed the room in a blue glow; he searched for a clear channel, but the screen remained a sea of pulsing static behind which vague figures swam in surreal distortion, auras without source. He stripped the

bed and wetted a thin, rough towel with warm water and
began to wipe the vomit off the girl's face, off her hard,
shallow chest, off her stomach as it rose and fell with each
breath. "Feels good," she said. Jones rinsed the towel and
continued the ablution, working down her stick-thin legs
and then turning her onto her stomach, massaging the tepid
towel over her back and buttocks, along her thighs. The
curtains fluttered, parting like wings and rising into the
room. It was early, but the sun was setting in the valley,
the brown rim of hills holding a halo of bright light, an
emphatic, contoured seam of gold, and different sounds —
the screeching of tires, the jangling of keys, a dog bark-
ing — began to carry clearly, sounds so ordinary and near
they seemed to have a source, not within the room, not
out in the world, but in memory.

When the girl sank into sleep, Jones slipped out into
the hallway.

"Your wife?" McKillop asked.

"Just a girl I picked up."

"Jesus, man." With forced jocularity, the doctor
slapped Jones on the back. "You know how to pick them."

Out on the street dusk settled, a moment of suspen-
sion. The sky was still deep blue with a weak edge of white
draining away in the west. An Indian crouched on the curb
outside the motel, his face brown and puckered like a
windfall apple in autumn.

Jones and McKillop entered a bar next door.

"I'm taking her to a hospital," Jones said.

"There's precious little a hospital can do," the doctor
said. "Let's have a drink here," he called out. "They'll

start a morphine drip. It'll keep her euphoric until she dies."

"Then I'll send her home," Jones said. In the navy he'd learned one thing, and for Jones it amounted to a philosophy: there was no real reason to go forward, but enormous penalties were paid by those who refused. He'd learned this lesson rubbing Brasso into his belt buckle and spit shining his boots for inspections that never came. "I could leave right now," he said. "I could drive away."

"Why don't you," the doctor said. "Turn tail, that's what I'd do." He ordered boilermakers and drank his by dumping the shot of bourbon into the schooner of beer. He polished off his first drink and called for another round.

"Deep down," McKillop said, "I'm really shallow."

Jones said, "I had this feeling if I kept driving everything would be okay."

"The healing, recuperative powers of the West," the doctor said. "Teddy Roosevelt and all that. The West was a necessary invention of the Civil War, a place of harmony and union. From the body politic to the body —"

Jones only half listened. He found himself resisting the doctor's glib reductions.

"I'd like to hit the road," McKillop was saying. The phrase had an antiquated sound. Even in the cool of the bar, McKillop was sweating. He pressed a fat finger down on a bread crumb, then flicked it away.

"You looked bad when you saw her," Jones said.

"I'll be all right," McKillop said. He downed his drink. "I'm feeling better now. You'll need help, but I'm not your doctor."

McKillop bought a roll of quarters and made a few sloppy calls to friends in Seattle, waking them, demanding favors for the sake of old times, invoking old obligations, twice being told to fuck off and finally getting through to an old resident friend at Mercy Hospital, who said he'd look at the girl if nothing else could be done.

"We'll take care of her," McKillop said to Jones. They walked down to the section of windowless warehouses and blank-faced cold-storage buildings, walked along cobbled streets softly pearled with blue lamplight, apple crates stacked up twenty, thirty feet high against the brick. Beyond the train tracks, the Columbia flowed quietly; a path of cold moonlight stretched across the water like a bridge in a dream, the first step always there, at Jones's feet. Through crate slats Jones saw eyes staring, men slumped in the boxes for the night, out of the wind, behind a chinking of newspaper, cardboard, fluttering plastic. Jones stopped. A canvas awning above a loading dock snapped in the breeze like a doused jib sail.

"Don't you worry, Jonesy boy," the doctor said. "We'll get her squared away. Tomorrow, in Seattle." He reached into his bag and handed Jones a vial and a syringe. "If it gets too much, the pain, you know, give her this. Only half, four or five milligrams. You can do it, right? Just find a vein."

A fire burned on the banks of the river. A circle of light breathed out and the shadows of stone-still men danced hilariously. A woman walked through the grass outside the circle; her legs were shackled by her own pants, blue jeans dropped down around her ankles; she stumbled, stood, stumbled, struggled. "I know what you want," she shouted back at the circle of men. "I know what you want." She fell, laughing hideously.

The doctor was clutching Jones's hand, squeezing and shaking it, and Jones got the idea that the doctor might never let go.

Outside the motel, the same wrecked Indian stood and approached Jones. His left cowboy boot was so worn down around the heel that the bare shoe tacks gave a sharp metallic click on the cement with each crippled step. He blinked and thrust a hand at Jones.

"My eyes hurt when I open 'em," he said. "And they hurt when I close 'em. All night I don't know what to do. I keep opening and closing my eyes."

Jones reached into his pocket and pulled a rumpled dollar loose from his wad of muster pay.

"I swear," the Indian said. "Somebody's making my eyes go black."

Jones gave him the bone. He tried to see in the man the facial lines of an Eskimo, but his skin was weathered, the lines eroded.

"SoHappy," he said.

"Me too," Jones said.

"No," the Indian said, thumping his chest. "So-Happy. Johnny SoHappy, that's me. Fucking me."

He blinked and backed away, wandering off alone, shoe tacks roughly clawing the sidewalk.

The girl was awake, shrouded in white sheets, staring at the ceiling, her breathing shallow but regular. Jones lay in the bed beside her, suffering a mild case of the spins. The walls turned, soft and summery, like the last revolution of a carousel wobbling to a stop. He looked out the window. Under the moonlight each leaf on the apple tree was a spoonful of milk.

Jones felt the girl's dry, thin fingers wrap around his wrist like a bird clutching at a perch.

"I love you," she whispered. Her voice was hoarse and frightening.

Jones shut his eyes against the spinning room. The movement crept beneath his closed lids, and Jones opened his eyes, to no effect. The room continued to spin.

"How about you, Jones? You could just say it, I wouldn't care if it wasn't the truth. Not anymore."

Jones pressed her hand lightly.

"Where are we, Jones?" she asked. "I mean, really. What's the name of this place?"

They were a long way from Carbondale, from the home he'd seen the night they left. An oak tree hiding the collapsing remains of a childhood fort, a frayed rope with knotted footholds dangling from the hatch, a sprinkler turning slowly over the grass, a lounge chair beneath a sun shade, a paper plate weighted against the wind by an empty cocktail glass.

"I'm hot," she said.

Jones lifted her out of bed. She was hot, but she wasn't sweating. Against his fingers, her skin felt dry and powdery, friable, as if the next breeze might blow it all away, and he'd be left holding a skeleton. He wrapped her in a white sheet. She hooked her arms around his neck, and Jones carried her, airy as balsa, into the aqueous green light of the hallway and down the steps.

"Where we going?" she asked.

The surface of the pool shimmered, smooth as a turquoise stone. Jones unwrapped the sheet and let it fall. The girl was naked underneath.

"Hold on," Jones said.

He walked down the steps at the shallow end, the water washing up around his ankles, his knees, his waist, and then he gently lowered the girl until her back floated on the surface.

"Don't let go," she said, flinching as she touched water. In panic, she gasped for air.

"I won't," Jones said. "Just relax."

Her skin seemed to soak in water, drink it up like a dehydrated sponge, and she felt heavier, more substantial. Her arms and legs grew supple, rising and falling in rhythm to the water. He steered her around the shallow end.

"Except in songs on the radio," she said, "nobody's ever said they love me."

Her eyes were wide and vacant, staring up through the leaves of the apple tree, out past them into the night sky, the moon, the vault of stars.

"You think anybody's watching us?" the girl asked.

Jones looked up at the rows of darkened rooms surrounding the pool. Here and there a night-light glowed. Air conditioners droned.

"I doubt it," he said.

She let her arms spread wide and float on the surface as Jones eased her toward the edge of the pool. He lifted her out and set her down on the sheet. At the deep end of the pool, below the diving board, he saw the lounge chair, its yellow webbing and chrome arms shining in the beams of underwater light. He took a deep breath and dove in. The water was as warm as the air, easing the descent from one element to the next. Jones crept along the bottom until he found the chair. Pressure rang in his ears, and a dizziness spread through him as he dragged it along the length of the pool. For a moment he wanted to stop, to stay on the bottom and let everything go black; he held himself until every cell in his blood screamed and the involuntary instincts of his body craving air drove him back up and he surfaced, his last breath exploding out of him. He set the chair against the apple tree.

They sat beneath the tree while Jones caught his breath. A hot wind dried their skin.

"I liked Little Bighorn the best," the girl said.

"It was okay." Jones watched a leaf float across the pool. "You really think he's looking for you?"

"I know he is," she said. "He's got all his buddies on the police force that are saved — you know, born again."

"You want to go back there?"

The girl was quiet, then she said, "Weekends Dad and them hunt around under bridges by rivers, looking for graffiti with satanic messages. For devil worship you need the four elements. You need earth, wind, fire, and water. That's what he says. So they look by rivers, and maybe they see some graffiti, or they find an old chicken bone, and they think they really got themselves something."

It seemed an answer, wired through biblical circuitry.

"Tomorrow you're going to a hospital," Jones said. "The doctor arranged it. Everything's set."

He carried the girl upstairs and placed her on the bed. In five weeks she'd gone from a girl he'd picked up in the heartland to an old woman, her body retreating from the world, shrunken and curled and lighter by the hour, it seemed. Her hair had never grown back, and the ulcerations from early chemo treatments had so weakened her gums that a tooth had come loose, falling out, leaving a black gap in a smile that should have been seductive to the young boys back in Carbondale. The whites of her eyes had turned scarlet red. Her limbs were skeletal, fleshless and starved. She'd said she was eighteen, but now she could have passed for eighty.

"You think I'll go to hell?"

"Probably."

"Jones —"

"Well, why do you talk like that?"

"I don't know." She clutched the sheet around her neck. "When I open my mouth these things just come out. They're the only words I have."

"One of my tours," Jones said, "we were on maneuvers in the Mediterranean." A boiler exploded, he said, and a man caught fire in a pool of burning oil. Crazed, aflame, engulfed, the man ran in erratic circles on the deck, a bright, whirling light in the darkness, shooting back and forth like an errant Roman candle, while other men chased him, half-afraid to tackle the man and catch fire themselves. Finally, beyond all hope, out of his mind, the man jumped over the deck railing, into the sea. "You

could hear the flames whipping in the wind as he fell,"
Jones said. "Then he was gone. It was the sorriest thing
I ever witnessed." Afterwards, he'd helped extinguish the
fire, and for doing his duty he'd been awarded a dime-sized
decoration for heroism.

"Everywhere we go," she said, and there was a long
pause as her breath gurgled up through lungs full of fluid,
"there's never any air-conditioning."

Jones held her hand, a bone. He thought she coughed
this time, but again she was only trying to breathe. Suddenly he did not want to be in bed beside her. But he
couldn't move.

"The Eskimos live in ice huts," he said.

"Sounds nice right now."

"It's very cold," Jones continued.

"I wish we were going there."

The girl coughed, and then curled into a fetal ball.
"It's like hot knives stabbing me from inside," she said.

Jones lifted himself from the bed. He turned on the
bedside lamp and took the morphine and the syringe from
his shirt pocket. "The first explorers thought Eskimos
roamed from place to place because they were poor," he
said. "They thought the Eskimos were bums." He ripped
the cellophane wrapper from the syringe and pushed the
needle into the vial, slowly drawing the plunger back until
half the clear liquid had been sucked into the barrel. "They
were always on the move," he said. The girl bit into the
pillow until her gums bled and left an imprint of her mouth
on the case. Her body had an alertness, a tension that
Jones sensed in the tortured angles she held her arms at,

the faint weak flex of her atrophied muscles. She raised her head and opened her mouth wide, her startled red eyes searching the room as if to see where all the air had gone. "But when you think about it, you understand that it's efficient." Jones pushed the air bubbles out of the syringe until a drop of morphine beaded like dew at the tip of the needle. "Movement is the only way for them to survive in the cold. Even their morality is based on the cold, on movement." Jones now continued speaking only to dispel the silence and the lone sound of the girl's labored breathing. He unclenched her hand from the sheets and bent her arm back, flat against the bed. "They don't have police," he said, "and they don't have lawyers or judges. The worst punishment for an Eskimo is to be left behind, to be left in the cold." Inspecting her arm, he found the widest vein possible and imagined it flowing all the way to her heart and drove the needle in.

McKillop had taken the girl's purse and dumped the contents on the bed. He rummaged through it, and found a blue gumball, safety pins, pennies, a shopping list, and several pamphlets from which he read. "Listen," he said. " 'For centuries lovers of God and of righteousness have been praying: Let your kingdom come. But what is that kingdom that Jesus Christ taught us to pray for? Use your Bible to learn the who, what, when, why, and where of the Kingdom.' " He laughed. "Ironic, huh?"

"We don't know, do we?" Jones said.

"Oh come on," the doctor said. He took up a scrap of notepaper. "Blush. Lipstick — Toffee, Ruby Red. Two pair white cotton socks. Call Carolyn."

"Stay out of her stuff," Jones said.

"I was looking for ID," he said. "What's her name?"

Jones thought for a moment and then said, "It's better that you don't know."

"You didn't OD her, did you?"

"No," Jones said. Once last night he'd woken to the sound of the girl's voice, calling out. She spoke to someone who was not in the room and began to pick invisible things out of the air. Watching her struggle with these phantoms had made Jones feel horribly alone. Delirious, she ended by singing the refrain of a hymn. He said to the doctor, "I thought about it though."

"You could tell the truth. It's rather unsavory, but it's always an option."

Jones looked at the doctor. "It's too late," he said.

"I've tried the truth myself, and it doesn't work that well anyway. Half the time, maybe, but no more. What good is that? The world's a broke-dick operation. The big question is, who's going to care?"

"Her family," Jones said. "Born-again Christians."

"I was raised a Catholic." McKillop pulled a silver chain from around his neck and showed Jones a tarnished cross. "It was my mother's religion. I don't believe, but it still spooks me."

"This is against the law."

"If you sent her home, there'd be questions."

"There'll be questions anyway," Jones said. "Her stepdad's a fanatic. He'll be looking for me. He believes in what he's doing, you know?"

"I vaguely remember believing —"

"Not everything has to do with you," Jones said. He

felt the sadness of language, the solitude of it. The doctor had no faith beyond a system of small ironies; it was like trying to keep the rain off by calling to mind the memory of an umbrella.

The doctor had dispensed with the nicety of a flask and now drank straight from the bottle.

"Never made it home last night," McKillop said.

"You look it," Jones said.

"I got lucky," McKillop said. "Sort of." He wiped his lips and said, "I wish I had a doughnut." He pulled a green apple from his pocket, buffing it on the lapel of his wrinkled jacket. He offered the bottle to Jones. Jones shook his head. "I'd watched this woman for a long time, desired her from afar, and then suddenly there I was, in bed with her, touching her, smelling her, tasting her. But I couldn't get it up."

"Maybe you should stop drinking."

"I like drinking."

"It's not practical," Jones said.

"Quitting's a drastic measure," McKillop said. He took a bite of the apple. "For a man who gets lucky as little as I do."

"I'll see you," Jones said.

III

By afternoon he had crossed the bridge at Deception Pass and driven south and caught a ferry to Port Townsend. He drove west along 101 and then veered north, hugging the shoreline of the Strait of Juan de Fuca, passing through Pysht and Sekiu, driving until he hit Neah Bay and the

Makah Reservation, when finally there was no more road. It had remained hot all the way west, and now a wildfire burned across the crown of a mountain rising against the western verge of the reservation. The sky turned yellow under a pall of black smoke. Flecks of ash sifted like snow through the air. White shacks lined either side of the street, staggering forward on legs of leaning cinder block, and a few barefoot children played in the dirt yards, chasing dust devils. Several girls in dresses as sheer and delicate as cobwebs stood shielding their eyes and staring at the fire. Sunlight spread through the thin fabric, skirts flickering in the wind, so that each of the young girls seemed to be going up in flames.

Jones moved slowly through town, raising a trail of white dust, which mingled with the black ash and settled over the children, the shacks, a scattering of wrecked cars, and then along the foot of the mountain he followed an eroded logging road until it too vanished. A yellow mobile home sat on a bluff, and behind it, hidden by a brake of wind-crippled cedar, was the ocean. Jones heard the surf and caught the smell of rough-churned sea. A man in overalls came out of the mobile home — to Jones, he looked like an Eskimo. Jones switched off the ignition. The car rocked dead, but for a moment he felt the pressure of the entire country he'd crossed at his back, the vibration of the road still working up through the steering column, into his hands and along his arms, becoming an ache in his shoulders, a numbness traveling down his spine. Then the vibrations stopped, and he felt his body settle into the present.

Jones got out of the car. The man hooked a thumb in his breast pocket, the ghost habit of a smoker. Behind

cracked lips, his teeth were rotten. He watched a retrofit
bomber sweep out over the ocean, bank high and round,
and circle back over the hill, spraying clouds of retardant.
The chemicals fell away in a rust-red curtain that closed
over the line of fire.

"How'd it start?" Jones asked.

"Tiny bit of broken bottle will start a fire, sun hits
it right." The man lit a cigarette. "Been a dry summer.
They logged that hill off mostly, and don't nobody burn
the slash. Where you headed?"

Jones said he was just driving.

"Used to be a love colony down there," the man said.
He pointed vaguely toward the ocean. "You get the hippies
coming back now and again, looking for the old path down.
But the trails all growed over." The man ran his tongue
over the black gum between missing front teeth. "I thought
maybe you was one of them."

"No," Jones said. "Never been here before."

"You can park, you want," he said. "There's a game
trail runs partways down."

"Thanks."

"You'll see the old Zellerbach mill."

He found the abandoned mill in ruin, a twisted heap
of metal. He sat on a rusted flume and pulled a patch of
burnt weeds from the foundation. With a stick he chipped
at the hard, dry ground and dug out three scoops of loose
dirt, wrapping them in one of the girl's shirts. When he
finished, he sat against a stump, counting the growth rings
with his finger until near heartwood he'd numbered two
hundred years.

*   *   *

A clamshell chime chattered like cold teeth beneath the awning of a bait shop. Inside the breakwater, boats pulled at their moorings. Jones walked up and down the docks of the marina until he found a Livingston slung by davits to the deck of a cabin cruiser. The windows of the cruiser were all dark, canvas had been stretched across the wheelhouse, and the home port stenciled across the stern was Akutan. He lowered the lifeboat into the water, pushed off, and let himself drift quietly away from the marina.

When he'd rowed out into the shipping lane, Jones pull-started the twenty-horse Evinrude, and followed a flashing red beacon out around the tip of Cape Flattery to the ocean. He kept just outside the line of breaking waves, hugging the shore, the boat tossed high enough at times along the crest of a swell to see a beach wracked with bone gray driftwood. Jones pulled the motor and rode the surf until the hull scraped sand. He loaded the girl into the boat, up front for ballast.

He poled himself off the sand with the oar and then rowed. Each incoming wave rejected his effort, angling the bow high and pushing the boat back in a froth of crushed white foam. Finally he managed to cradle the boat in the trough between breaking waves. The motor kicked out of the water with a high-rev whine, and Jones steered for open sea, heading due west. Beyond the edge of the shelf, the rough surface chop gave way to rolling swells, and Jones knew he was in deep water. He'd forgotten how black a night at sea was, how even the coldest, dying star seemed near and bright in the dark. He became afraid and drew the world in like a timid child, trembling with unreasonable fears — the terrible life below him, the girl's stepfather and his fanatic pursuit, his own fugitive life in flight from this moment. If it became history he would be judged and found guilty. Spindrift raked over the bow, splashing his face. The sea heaved in a sleepy rhythm. He crossed the black stern of a containership at anchor, four or five stories of high wall, and when he throttled back to a dead drift he heard voices from the deck top, human voices speaking in a language he did not understand.

He ran another mile and cut the engine. The round world was seamless with the night sky, undivided, the horizon liquid and invisible except for a spray of stars that flashed like phosphorescence, rising out of the water. A cool breeze whispered over the surface. August was over. He'd piled the sleeping bag with beach rocks, and then he'd cleaned the car of evidence, collected the souvenirs, the trinkets, the orange smiles, the wig, and stuffed them down into the foot of the bag, knotting it shut with nylon rope. He'd taken the Bible, opened it to the genealogy, and scratched the month and year into the margins. Jones considered the possibility, as he rocked in the trough of a swell, that all this would one day break free from its deep hold in the sea, wash to the surface, the bumper stickers from Indian battles and decals commemorating the footpaths and wagon trails of explorers and pioneers, the resting places of men and women who'd left their names to towns and maps. And then the girl herself, identified by her remains, a story told by teeth and bones, interpreted.

Jones looped a rope tether around the handle of his flashlight and tied the other end to the sleeping bag. He checked the beam, which shone solidly in the darkness, a wide swath of white light carved out of the air. He unpackaged the soil he'd collected from the collapsed mill and sprinkled it across the sleeping bag, spreading earth from head to foot. It seemed a paltry ritual — the dirt, the light — but he was determined to observe ceremony. With his tongue he licked away a coating of salt from the rim of his lips. His hands were growing cold and stiff. He hoisted the head end of the bag over the port side and then pivoted the girl's feet around until the whole bag pitched overboard. Jones held it up a final instant, clutching the flashlight, allowing the air bubbles to escape, and then let go. Down she swirled, a trail of light spinning through a sea that showed green in the weakening beam and then went black. In silence Jones let himself drift until, borne away by the current, he could no longer know for certain where she'd gone down.

Back within the breakwater, Jones tied the lifeboat with a slack line to a wooden cleat. The mountain had vanished from view, swallowed by darkness, but a prevailing westerly had blown the wildfire across its crown, and a flare of red yellow flame swept into the sky. An old Makah trudged up the road, dragging a stick through the dust, leaning on it when he stopped to watch the hieroglyphic write itself in fire on the edge of the reservation. Jones sat on the dock, dangling his legs. Flakes of feathery black ash drifted through the air and fanned lightly against his face. Spume crusted and stung his lips, and he was thirsty. He listened to the rhythm of the water as it played an icy cool music in the cadenced clinking of ropes and pulleys and bell buoys. Out beyond the breakwater the red and green running lights of a sailboat appeared, straggling into port. The wind lifted the voices of the sailors and carried them across the water like a song. One of the sailors shouted, "There it is." He stood on the foredeck and pointed toward the banner of flames rising in the sky.

AMERICAN BULLFROG

NOW, it's a common and fond fantasy for children, and especially young boys, to nurture the idea that the strange, harsh, ridiculous, badly dressed people raising them are not their real parents, that some farcical mix-up attended the delivery, but when I was thirteen, fourteen, I liked my parents okay, and in truth it was them, my mom and dad, who seemed to be cooking up a little fantasy of their own, namely, that I was not their son. Almost overnight, their behavior became so unreasonable, and their understanding so thick, I couldn't for the life of me figure out what had gotten into them. I was especially puzzled because in the past they had always seemed fond of me. They pinned my good report cards to the fridge, or rested a baseball trophy atop the television, which let me know that, even though they believed bragging was among the worst of bad manners, they were fairly accepting of me, and didn't care who knew it. My mom in particular possessed an uncanny understanding of me, but even my dad, now and then, surprised me with his insight into my nature. On school mornings, for instance, he used to be able to touch my forehead with the back of his hand and know that I hadn't done my homework. "You don't have a fever," he would say, and it was as if he could feel my brains were cold and hadn't been used. Then, as I said, almost overnight, they both changed.

Their trouble seemed exacerbated when I decided that the only life for me was the life of an outlaw. In this I was greatly influenced by Claude Brown's book *Manchild in the Promised Land,* and to begin my career as a hooligan I stopped using the front door whenever practical. Instead I climbed the big maple that grew on the side of our house and shinnied across a limb to the window, where I was able, with a last, desperate, daring lunge, to grip ahold of the sill, squirm forward, and drop face first onto my bedroom floor. After a couple weeks of this my dad sat me down and asked: "What the fuck's wrong with the door!" Apparently, my dad had not read Claude Brown, nor was he much of a romantic, and he hated trouble of any sort, and in fact, with his job and the bills and his car worrying him to death all the time, he was starting to seem unimaginative and modest in his expectations of life. How could I explain to him that I needed to use the maple tree because we lived in a house that lacked an official tenement-slum fire escape? And how could I explain, without hurting his tetchy feelings, that using the front door lacked courage and dignity, the way I had to stop by the living room every night and detail where I'd been, who I was with, what we all did? Both my mom and dad had become so obtuse I really questioned their ability to understand even the simplest ideas, and by climbing up and down the tree I had hoped, among other things, to shield them from the pain of considering problems that were, it was clear to me, over their heads.

It was about this time that they began to discuss me in the third person. To give them credit, I suspect they did this in the belief that, by an effort of abstraction, they might at least begin to understand me as a concept. Like Platonists, they would grapple with the distant theory, before getting into the nearby particulars. But my mom and dad were not very logical. For instance, they bought big forty-pound boxes of powdered milk to save money. It wasn't even milk — white powder and tap water — and it was so lumpy I wouldn't drink it. So why, I would ask, buy it at all? *They* didn't drink it. Wasn't that a waste of money? They agreed, somewhat, and made me put away a glass a night, so as not to fritter away our hard-earned dollars. A forty-pound box of powder made five hundred gallons of milk, I calculated. I felt suicidal every time I opened the cupboard beneath the sink and saw the box. Anyway, it was their private comments, their little asides, that really clued me in to their new way of thinking. "He's not someone I know anymore," my mom said one night, and I can't tell you the ghostly feeling I got, hearing myself discussed as if I were some stranger, as if I had not lived in the same house with them for thirteen years — more than ample time to get to know a person.

More and more, they seemed moody and confused, driven to exasperation and irritability. What could account for this radical change? I took to marking the gallon jug of Cribari red with a pencil, and began making a census of the Olys in the fridge, just to gauge how much was getting drunk on a daily basis. And when I showered — once every three days, for the energy crisis was on and we were trying our best to conserve hot water, among other things — I counted out the blue-and-white Tuanals in the medicine chest. I even read their checkbook ledger. My survey wasn't science, of course, but it seemed to me that every-thing — the alcohol, the drugs, the money — was disap-pearing at the usual rate. I became worried that the problem was deeper, and grew concerned for their sanity.

To spare them the strain, I started watching what I'd say at home. Also, I began to avoid them. In addition to climbing in and out of our house by way of the tree, I kept to myself, or hung out in the alley, the park, the ravine, with my friends, in whom I found a more intelligent and understanding audience. So as not to appear conspicuous in this new world, I favored an unkempt, wild look. For-merly I had tried to look like my dad, but now it was necessary to quit combing Dippity-Do into my hair because somebody at school told me it looked faggy. Also I gave up my razor and grew the beginning of a mustache that was a source of hilarity to my sister, Janie. "When are you going to shave?" she asked one night. As far as I could see, all Janie had learned in three years of university was that, in matters concerning intellect, food, art, music, movies, fashion, and home decor, she was better than us. She only came home once a week, on Thursday nights, to eat dinner and make derogatory remarks. (Obviously, she was having her own fantasy, too.) Anyway, when Janie gave me the snotty business about my mustache, which I was rather tentative about anyway, and hadn't even decided yet whether or not it was turning out ugly, I became wild with shame and rage. Fortunately, I remembered a comeback Hopper had used, and snapped at her, "When you shave the beard between your legs!" Mom dropped her hamburger flipper and slapped my ear. In my life, she'd needed to hit me just twice before. The first time was for pretend-cooking a pot roast in the sandbox, and the second time was for drowning my cousin's baby chicken in a mason jar. This was the third time, and a charm. With the force of a great revelation it dawned on me that your real outlaws understood how intolerable and hopeless it was and never, under any circumstances, lived at home.

That night, with my ear still stinging, I ran upstairs, grabbed my coat, and climbed out the window. I swung down through the tree to the point where the trunk forked, and then hugged my way up the opposite branch, into Regimbal's bedroom. He was my best friend and he climbed in and out of his bedroom window too. Actually, we shared the same tree.

"Regimbal," I shouted, rapping on his window. "Open up."

"Hey," he said.

"I ran away," I told him. "Let me in."

I somersaulted into his bedroom.

"You didn't go very far," he said.

"It just happened a minute ago," I said. "Can I stay?"

"Did you really run away?"

"I can't stand it over there," I said. "That house is full of kooks."

"You know your dad'll call my dad."

Although his parents had always been rather dense and clumsy, their attitude toward Regimbal had begun to change, for the worse, just like with my mom and dad. I believe our parents had discussed us together and, as you often find in other kinds of ignorance, only reinforced one another's bigotries. It was contagious.

"You're right," I said. "I'll go stay in the park."

"There's homos in the park."

"I'm not afraid of a homo."

"Maybe you *are* a homo," Regimbal said.

"No fucking way," I said. "Close the drapes."

We stayed in his room awhile, smoking pine needles rolled in toilet paper and igniting piles of saltpeter on the windowsill. All this time we listened to Neil Young, loud. *See the lonely boy, out on the weekend* — man, that album kicked ass! I'd never had the experience of poignancy before, but I had it that night, and couldn't get enough of it. It was better than pot, which I'd tried but failed to get high on, and way better than the wine Regimbal and me made — for science credit! — out of Welch's grape, sugar, and yeast. Under its influence, I felt lost and lonely, as though my life had no bottom, and sad, too, and desperate, too, and nostalgic for a better time — at thirteen, I don't know how, but I had the idea life was better before I was born. I know it doesn't make sense, to wish you were alive before you were born, but anyway, that night, and for a long time afterwards, I became like a poignancy freak, an addict for the stuff, it was so strong, and when I wasn't getting a proper dose, when I wasn't feeling emotionally connected to a better life, when I wasn't feeling all sad and desirous and shitty and angry, I suffered withdrawal and bemoaned my lowly status and planned revenges on the indifferent world.

"Hey, scrotum."

I turned around to see Hopper and, farther back in the shadows, Riles. It was later that night, about eight o'clock, and me and Regimbal were out in the alley, shooting hoops under the blue flood lamp mounted on our garage. It was drizzling and mildly miserable but sometimes, when you run away, that's the chance you take, that the weather won't be on your side, either.

"What're you pussies up to?" Hopper said.

"He ran away," Regimbal said.

Riles hissed. He was famous in the neighborhood for overdosing on some kind of horse tranquilizer and surviving. He never had much to say. He was more the silent type. He had curly black hair and blue eyes, one of which wandered, and did its own thing, gazing at the sky, or at a tree behind you, floating around loose in his head, dumb as a guppy. When I first met him the eye was disorienting, but now I had learned a trick, and centered my attention, whenever necessary, by talking to his nose.

"I think you should leave your backyard, if you're gonna run away," Hopper said. "Where you plan to go?"

"I don't know," I said. I found myself enjoying the attention. "I'm just getting the fuck out of here."

"We're having a keg tomorrow. You girls want to come?"

"Where at?" I said.

"Carbone's old house."

I looked at Regimbal, raising my eyebrows. For a long time we had been developing the idea of hanging out with Hopper and Riles, older boys who drove jacked-up cars, swore freely, drank Mad Dog, and smoked in the alley, but they had, historically, despised us as toady immature camp followers. I felt about Hopper something nearly as moony and goo-goo as love. He was a senior at our school, Jesuit High, where we were frosh. I had watched him, studied him, imitated his clothes, his hairstyle, the things he said and the way he said them. In fact, it occurred to me, he was part of the reason I was running away.

"I told my sister to shave the beard between her legs."

"What for?" Hopper said. He lit a cigarette. "Well?"

"What time?" I said.

Hopper shrugged. "One, two, after your classes. Whenever you show up. We'll need some money for the keg. I'll meet you at school tomorrow, okay?"

Just then I heard my dad's leather slippers slapping on the walkway and before I could run the gate opened.

"There you are," he said. He nodded to Regimbal, and stared hard at Hopper and Riles. "Your dinner's getting cold."

"I'm not coming home," I said.

"Oh," my dad said. "Why's that?"

I shrugged. My dad reached into the pocket of his pork pants and pulled out his money clasp. He peeled loose a bill.

"That'll keep you," he said. "At least for a day."

The next morning, I yelled up to Regimbal's window, but his mom, his stepmom, came out on the back porch and told me to cut it out. "Can't you please just knock on the door?" she said. Carol Ann was at her wit's end, she had told us. Still, I thought she was kind of interesting. You could see in the frank daylight the furry hair on her face and shrivel lines around her lips that drew her mouth closed like a cloth purse. And the fan of lines at the corners of her eyes and her mouth were like strings crucial to working her smile, a smile that seemed to be operated, somehow, by her ears. Despite these ravages, from the sixties she had preserved a hairstyle like a child's drawing of a bird, and also a thick layer of makeup that made her seem stubborn, as if insistently waiting for the day when the world would again match the expression on her face. She had fake fingernails as big as peanut shells. Her interest in style was what intrigued me. My own mother eschewed style in favor of saving money, which made her seem both superior and irrelevant, female-wise, like a nun. Regimbal's mom was sexy, with a certain flavor of ruin.

Carol Ann was drinking a cup of joe, as she called it, and twiddling a lit cigarette between her creased, carroty fingers. I was thinking I should try to engage her in some light, distracting bullshit when I heard the branches of the tree shaking above my head, and saw Regimbal's feet and legs coming out like a breech birth as he backed out his window. He was kicking the empty air, trying and failing and then finding the first step.

"What the hell is wrong with you two?" Carol Ann shook her head, flapping her winged hair. "Freddie, I told you last time you did that I'd have your father board up the window. And now I'm gonna do it, I swear. You too," she said, turning on me. "I'm calling your mom and by tonight both you boys will have plywood over your windows. No shit. Don't laugh. Goddamn it, Freddie, don't laugh at me!"

Regimbal fell out of the tree.

"Remember, Mom, there's a dance tonight," he said.

We ditched through the fence and up the alley.

Regimbal crunched down on his head a goofy duck-cloth cap that he liked for some reason. He was shorter than me, a kind of squdgy, small kid who, to force an ersatz adolescence, had taken up weightlifting, which had had an unwanted, unforeseen, unfortunate effect, causing his neck to disappear, so he looked even denser, smaller. He had green eyes sunk back in shadowy, purple sockets and a heavy lower jaw and jutting lips like a lingcod. He wasn't handsome and, historically speaking, he breathed through his nose until, in annoyance, you hit him.

"I got eight dollars and change," I said, showing the money I had left from what Dad gave me.

"I couldn't find any money," Regimbal said, "so I grabbed these."

He reached into his pocket and held a fist of food stamps in his tiny hand, a five, a ten, some ones, purple and orange bills like play money from a game.

"I don't think Hopper'll take those."

"We'll see," Regimbal said, and we started for school. He had a box of Goobers and offered me some.

"What time is it?"

"I don't know. Nine like."

"I'm gonna call Diane," I said, ducking into a pay phone at the gas station.

"Finklebien? Why? She's a fat pig."

It was true, Diane Finklebien was chubby, but something about her — the fact that she wasn't real pretty, a kind of unhappy-looking, lagging-behind, unprotected, and weak member of the herd — gave me the thought that I could screw her. She was vulnerable. I don't know why, exactly, but I had the idea only clever boys and stupid girls had sexual relations, and I assumed anyone who would kiss me had to be an idiot. A year before, at our eighth-grade graduation party, she had gotten a bit silly on Boone's Farm, stood on her tippytoes, and kissed me in a way that I felt indicated severe desperation.

"Diane?" I said into the phone. "You want to go to a keg?"

"Sure," she said. "Who is this?"

"John. John Torrence. The keg's at Carbone's old house. You know where that is?"

She did, and it was taken care of.

After I hung up, Regimbal was pissed and gloomy. He said, "Haggis better not tell me to put a smile on my face today."

Haggis, our biology teacher, was something of a mad scientist. He was raising a forest of giant sequoias in milk cartons, which he planned to transplant, that summer, in California. A thousand years after I'm dead and gone, he'd told us, those trees'll be five hundred feet tall. Breathing, he'd said, breathing.

*　　　*　　　*

Our frogs felt like dill pickles from standing around all year in jars of formaldehyde. Me and Regimbal took them over to our station. We stood side by side at the dissecting table. I was flunking some classes. I was flunking biology. I couldn't get ahold of it to save my life. We'd been dissecting things all year, but the difference between an earthworm's pharynx and gizzard was something I couldn't keep straight. Once a specimen was cut open, everything inside just looked like sandwich spread to me. This was the biggie, too, the grand finale and coup de grâce of dissection, *Rana catesbeiana,* the American bullfrog, whose anatomy Mr. Haggis said, in a voice that always put me in mind of the word "hallelujah," would give us a good idea of the main features of human anatomy. But he'd said that about the cricket and the worm too.

"Check out the window," I said. "See if Hopper's outside."

"Nah," said Regimbal, after a quick look.

It seemed a good idea to turn the frog over on its back, which I did, pinning its pale white legs wide apart on the dissecting pan. The frog was dead, of course, but I felt pity for it anyway. As soon as I cut it open, it would resemble everything else. The one thing I'd learned in biology was that all this noise about how inside we're each one of us unique and special was bull, and that it was the outside, with the warty skin and webbed feet and the itty-bitty hands that had knuckles, and the slitty nares, and the pale, speckled air sac, and so on and so on, that made a thing its own self. Outside, you could identify what was a frog and what was a salamander; inside — sandwich spread.

Regimbal studied his frog. He worked its rubbery elbows and its little fingers spread out: "Hello, hello."

Regimbal asked, "Is yours a boy or a girl?"

I lifted it up close to my face, expecting to see a tiny frog pecker, something that looked like mine except green. Frogs were ancient, they were prehistoric, they'd been hopping around in swamps and trees for millions of years, this very frog had probably had ancestors who were stepped on by dinosaurs, but the more I looked at mine, the more alien and unnatural it seemed.

"What's yours?" I asked, but Haggis cruised by and Regimbal didn't answer.

"Smile, Regimbal," Haggis said.

Regimbal made a cut, which burped a little methane stink. Then he was a haywire butcher. I believe he didn't have the dimmest idea what he was pulling out of his frog, whether he was getting the parts whole or chopping them down into bits and pieces. Very quickly he gutted it, and what he had before him was a kind of frog coin purse, a scraped-out empty frog bag. He spread the chunks out across the table, nudged them with his scalpel. Lungs, stomach, intestines, the precardial sac — a term I remembered for some reason — which contained the heart? He tried to fool me by putting a Goober in his empty frog. "Christ, what's this?" he asked, working the chocolate peanut loose with a tweezer.

"What time is it?" I asked.

"We got about fifteen minutes left," Regimbal said. "Aren't you going to do your frog?"

It was true, I hadn't touched my frog.

"This is the heart," Regimbal said, stabbing a piece of his frog, "and this is the chow mein."

"What's wrong, Torrence?" Haggis said.

"I didn't study," I admitted. I noticed that the prospect of the party, of the beer and Diane, had a tonic effect on me. I didn't care so much what happened during class. I felt stoic. "I didn't want to ruin a perfectly good frog," I said.

We waited outside school for two hours, but Hopper and Riles never showed up. We hustled up Fifteenth to the Safeway and started to nickel-and-dime the food stamps, something Regimbal's dad taught us, sending us to the store after school to break the bills down and bring back the accumulated change, so he could return later and buy beer, cigarettes, toilet paper, and soap. Regimbal's dad was one of many thousands of men laid off at Boeing and worked odd off-the-books carpentry jobs at our church, and for other parishes in the dioceses, and also groomed the baseball fields, raking the basepaths and chalking in the foul lines. He told my dad he aimed to chase work, to move Regimbal and Carol Ann to Grand Junction. Naturally, from listening to Mr. Regimbal, we both learned to hate Boeing. Fuck Boeing, we'd say now. Before, as kids, me and Regimbal had decided that his dad was better than mine, because he built airplanes, Boeing airplanes, which were the most important things in Seattle, and we loved to watch the jets soar, streaks of silver like airborne salmon in the ocean of blue sky. My dad was a schoolteacher, a job we both had a low opinion of. But now I think Regimbal was a little ashamed of his dad's circumstance, which, the way it works, was his too.

We got in the express line over and over and bought crap until we were chased out of the store by the manager, a thin queer shaking his feather duster at us. "Scoot, scoot," he said.

Regimbal got pissy. "Hey, we can shop here the same as anyone else."

"Get out," the guy said.

The pockets of our field jackets bulged with candy, potato chips, fruit pies, grape pop, apples and bananas, a package of lunch meat, the kind with green olives embedded in it.

"How much did you get?" I asked.

"Five-ten, five-twenty, one two three," Regimbal said, clinking coins in his palm. "Five dollars twenty-three cents. You?"

"Four-nineteen," I said.

We ran for Carbone's down Fifteenth, a broad avenue along the borders of which some dreaming developer, years ago, had planted palm trees. Tropical palms in Seattle — you never saw the crows in them. They looked natural enough in the rain, though, and it was soon going to rain hard.

"Do you want any of this food?" Regimbal asked.

"I'll have the pie I got," I said. "Why'd you get that baloney?"

"I just always wondered about it," he said. "It's all right, too."

"I bet Diane's already there."

"I don't see why you had to call her."

"Why not? You jealous?"

"There won't be any other girls there."

"There might be."

Carbone's old house was across the alley from ours. On Sundays after church my dad and Mr. Regimbal would sit on our back porch and argue about the changes in Seattle. Mr. Regimbal said like usual the average guy, meaning him, was going to get screwed in the butt. "Look at what happened to Carbone, for godsakes," he'd say. My dad, who was fairly average himself, was relieved to see the neighborhood improve, after years of neglect and decline, even though he admitted to Mr. Regimbal that, morally speaking, he was against homos. But Seattle was in the dumps. Boeing had by that fall laid off sixty thousand men, and a lot of the run-down houses in our neighborhood, first rented by hippies and then blacks, were now getting bought and fixed up nicely by queers. I'd got so I could identify a homo when I saw one. They seemed neat and clean but quite shy, as a people.

All the houses across the alley, the entire block fronting Fifteenth, had been condemned that fall, and during the day their boarded windows and lopsided porches and yards scrabbled over with blackberry vines gave the neighborhood a mean, blighted, toothless appearance, but at night, reduced to vague silhouettes, they looked cruel and romantic in a manly way, I thought, sort of raggedy and rotten, disheveled and proudly standing on their last legs, despite a serious beating. The houses were slated for demolition in the spring, to be replaced by condos — a word I had never heard before. When the construction sign first went up, it had sounded to me like people would be living inside birds.

We dropped through the window well, into Carbone's basement. We lit matches and followed the flickering light up the stairs. The living room was crammed with people I'd never seen before. Hopper stood in the kitchen next to the keg, holding a stack of plastic cups.

"We got the money," Regimbal said.

Hopper looked at all the change. "What's this, your piggy bank?"

"Give us cups," I said.

I drank one beer quickly and was surprised at the effect it had on my comprehension. After only two or three swallows, I felt quite friendly toward myself, and toward Regimbal, too, who seemed like the warmest, truest friend I'd ever have. I wanted to tell him the truth about something, anything, and put my arm around him, and said, "I slept in the car last night."

He pushed my arm away and we got into a rowdy, mock fight.

"What the hell for?" he asked.

"Because my sister's a bitch, that's why."

Someone had come in the night and put a blanket over me, a wool army surplus blanket.

"Shouldn't you go find your girlfriend?"

"She's not my girlfriend, Regimbal. You pussy."

He slapped my cheek. I set my cup down and gave him a hip check. His beer spilled on my head. Somebody kicked me in the back.

"Hey," I said.

"Hey what," somebody shouted in the dark.

We went off to fill our cups again. A tall, gangly red-haired kid whose face was so puffy with acne he looked like a salmonberry said the keg was getting low, so we drank two cups rapidly, and then filled another, pumping the tap and drawing a fourth beer that was mostly head. We bummed cigarettes and wandered around. Everybody was older than us, boys from the senior class at school, and some serious losers who'd graduated a year earlier. Burning cigarettes dotted the air, swept in orange circles through the black. Bongs bubbled away and the pine-scented blue smoke of hash drifted through the crowd. There wasn't hardly any space between people, and everyone walked with their beers hoisted like standards above their heads. With its windows boarded, the house was dark, except for a few candles.

"There's Valentine," Regimbal said, pointing to a brown-skinned Filipino boy sitting on a milk crate. "Did you know he's a pimp?"

"He's not a pimp," I said. People were always saying so-and-so was this, so-and-so was that. A girl I knew had a mother who was supposed to be a prostitute. The few times I'd been to her house, there was never any food or furniture, only shag rug and pillows and bottles of cold duck, but both her and her mom had closets full of ridiculously nice clothes, fancy things a normal person could find occasion to wear only once or maybe twice a year. They each had their own white telephone and two separate phone numbers. It was a little suspicious, but still, I didn't think it proved anything.

Regimbal dragged me over to Valentine.

"You wanna buy a woman?" he said.

"See?" Regimbal said. "Valentine, show us some pictures."

Valentine reached for his wallet, and slung an accordion folder, packed with pictures, at our faces. Most of the girls were our age or a little older. Some of them were white, and a good many were oriental. All of them were smiling.

I wasn't sure prostitutes smiled. I said, "These are like your sisters, right?"

"One of them is," Valentine said. He had a high-pitched nasal voice. "Ten bucks, if you want her," he said.

Now I didn't know what was going on. "Ten dollars?" I finished my fourth beer and achieved a state of drunkenness that surpassed all my previous experience. "Is that all?"

"Do you take food stamps?" Regimbal asked.

"Cash money," Valentine said. His slacks were pressed, his shirt was open to his belly, and his shoes were shined. He drew a long brown cigarette from a flat gold case. He lit the smoke with a quick flick of a matching lighter. He wore a massive ring on his finger and a gold chain around his neck. His fingernails were clean.

"You're not really a pimp," I said.

He shrugged. Regimbal said, "I told you he is."

I thought I heard Diane, thought I heard her say, "Acid? Are we taking acid?" but when I walked in the direction of her voice, I couldn't find her. Soon I had lost sight of Regimbal, of Hopper, of Riles, of anyone with a familiar face. My comprehension wasn't nearly as keen as it was earlier, and I no longer felt friendly toward myself, or anyone else. The place seemed full of strangers, all boys. I eddied around the edge of some boys, bohunk greasers and stoners from Renton, and one of the stoners was saying, "Now I got my own apartment. It's got everything. A kitchen, a bathtub with a shower in it. The furniture's already furnished. Before that I lived in a mental institution. 'Cause I said I was going to blow up my uncle's car. Before that I was in foster care. Before that I stayed with my granny. Before that I lived at home. Before that I wasn't born." I slid by those boys and headed upstairs, where I had the idea there would be light and, more importantly, air. The banister was broken, the spikes kicked out. The peeling, wet wallpaper showed a pattern of cordate olive-green leaves like a vine of unripe hearts. The creaky steps were crowded with boys. I kept stepping on people's hands, and out of the dark, beery pandemonium, people kept saying, Hey, fuck you. On the landing I discovered that my instincts had been right. Gray light and rain filtered through a hole in the roof.

I wandered down the hall and found a bathroom and pissed in the sink, for the growler was full of garbage. I saw Diane. She gripped my coat sleeve with her fat fingers and said, "I'm fucked, man."

We wandered through the upper floor, searching the different rooms, poking around. It looked as though the place had been picked clean by thieves. Everything was gone, right down to the people, except for a few small overlooked or lost or forgotten items — a mateless shoe, a black comb with a few snapped strands of hair still in the teeth.

"Things happened here," she said.

"What?"

"Stuff," she said. "Different stuff. Somebody read a book all night. I don't know. People lived here. It's creepy."

She reached for my hand and we went into Bobby Carbone's old room. Other than a mattress and a chair, there was no furniture. It was empty, and if we spoke, I knew our voices would echo. We kissed. Diane sat on the old mattress and drew her sweater up over her head. She sat there, neatly folding it, like a grown woman, in the dim gray light.

"Do you have any pot?" I asked.

"I'm already so fucking high," she said. "God, what would people say if they knew?"

"I don't know," I said.

"Normally I'd be, where would I be, normally?"

I watched her finish folding the sweater and set it aside on the floor. "Where's your beer?"

"Oh —"

"You're not that high."

"Huh?"

"You're not even drunk," I said. "You're faking."

"No I'm not! I'm buzzed, man. I am."

She took her bra off, like that was part of the argument. She had little plump breasts. I don't know what I was feeling, but I had an erection, nonetheless. I sat on the bed beside her and untied my boots. I yanked off my socks. They were soaked. They made me want to cry as I looked at them there, bunched on the floor, flat and gray as dead squirrels. I reached over and touched Diane's left breast. I held it. I couldn't feel anything. My hands were freezing. I was shaking. She shrank away from me. "It's cold," she said.

I finished undressing and climbed in with her. Then I got up and blocked the door with a chair. We lay there very quietly, not moving at all, but it didn't matter; I came immediately, on her leg.

"Whoops," she said.

She wiped her fingers over the silver trail on her thigh and then sniffed them. "It smells like mold," she said.

Her flesh was white and waxy, a cadaverous look that deepened the sense of cold I felt. Her lips were flecked with flaking pink lipstick and two cakey moons of blue arched above her eyes and a chickenpox scar sat square in the middle of her forehead. I made my fingers walk up her spine and through the light brown hair at the back of her neck, then down around her butt and over to a rust-colored scab that crusted at the tip of her elbow, then over to her breast, which was dotted on the side with two tiny moles.

My fingers walked all over her body and in the dark I touched the soft cold skin of her face as if I were a blind man looking for familiar features.

"Hello, hello," I said.

In a little while, I was ready again. I touched her pooty. I climbed on top of her. She took ahold of me and guided me in. It was clear right away that we weren't made for each other. The way she rocked and squirmed around, I was afraid I'd fall off, and decided that it was necessary to grab onto her head. I held onto her head with both hands, just above the ears, as if to the handle of a pogo stick. I dug my feet into the mattress for traction. Once I got arranged, though, I discovered that her mouth was way down by my Adam's apple. If I slid down to kiss her, I was afraid my penis would pop out. I couldn't figure what to do. I sucked on her forehead and could taste rain and apple-flavored shampoo in her hair. I think she must have felt the arrangement was no good too, because she was grabbing my butt, trying to keep me from sliding off. She strained her neck and tilted her head and opened her mouth like a baby bird, and thus managed to lick my chin. We wiggled some, and I kept digging my feet into the mattress, jumping forward, but Diane's efforts made her move one way, and my exertions made me move the opposite way, and I wanted to start all over again. I looked behind me, and watched my own butt go up and down. I could see why they called it humping. Her toenails were painted red. I tried doing it with my eyes closed. When I came I nearly ripped her ears off.

"Ouch," she said.

I got up.

"Don't go," Diane said. "Stay now."

This seemed very important to her. I lay down in that old damp rosin bag of a bed and waited. Bored, I closed my eyes and felt around, reached my finger inside her. Each finger, one at a time. For a long while we lay spooned in the springless sag of the mattress, breathing. When she wasn't looking, I sniffed my fingers, and then put them in my mouth and tasted them. Elephants, I thought, when I smelled my fingers. The previous summer I'd had a job mucking stalls and hosing down cages at the Woodland Park Zoo, a job I'd got by lying about my age. Diane smelled like the elephant cages, the smell of fresh wet straw just after sunrise.

"Are you hungry?" she said. In her voice there was something I'd never heard in a girl before, groggy and sweet, far away, as if she had picked up a slurry gentleness, a tenderness, in some other world beyond this damp little room.

"No," I said.

"We could go to IHOP."

"I said I'm not hungry. Besides I got all kinds of food in my coat."

"We could drink coffee. They give you a pitcher of it and you can stay as long as you want."

Suddenly, and surprisingly, I found myself appreciating my dad, who also lost his patience with my mom when she asked him questions, or tried to suggest fun activities.

"Don't worry," Diane said, "if I get pregnant I'll go to Alabama."

I hadn't even thought about birth control. "Alabama?"

"Everybody goes to Alabama to have their babies," she explained.

The idea of babies and Alabama put me off.

"Would I have to go?" I wondered.

"No," she said. "You go to Alabama by yourself. My cousin did, anyway."

"I have to go," I said. "I don't mean Alabama, I mean —"

I put on my socks, my underwear, etc. As I was tying my boots, I noticed Diane was crying. Just a trace of wet trailing across her cold white face.

"You want to go catch a movie sometime?" It was what my dad would say.

"When?" she asked. That was what my mom would say, pinning him down.

"Next week," I said, "or —"

"Sure."

"Great," I said.

I found Regimbal in one of the bedrooms. He broke his chocolate pie in half and shared it with Riles. They ran their pink tongues deep into the brown pudding. I needed to sit down.

"Where you been?" Regimbal said.

"What time is it?" I wanted to know.

"The keg's empty," Regimbal said. "We're gonna head over to the park."

"I might go home," I said. I would have sold my soul to the devil right then to get all that beer out of me.

"You're done running away, I guess," Regimbal said.

"I'm wasted," Riles said. "We should make a run up to the liquor store before we go to the park."

"I don't get it," I said.

"What?" Regimbal said. "Here, eat something."

"No way can I eat."

"We're gonna take some beers over to the park," Regimbal said.

"Are you drunk?"

"Yeah I'm drunk. You?"

"Yeah. Who all's going?"

"Just the main guys, me, Riles, Hopper, Page, some others."

I went over to the window and breathed the wet air through a crack in the boards. Across the alley I could see our house. By the arrangement of lights, I could tell that dinner was over, and that my mom sat in the kitchen, clipping coupons, and that my dad had gone to his room, where a blue light pulsed, to doze off in front of the television, watching the local news.

Downstairs the house was still thick with people, the air fugged and nasty, but when Hopper cruised through, announcing that the keg was empty, people began to leave, and someone kicked open the front door, letting in the clean, wet smell of rain and wind. I stepped out onto Carbone's old porch, and remembered the way Mr. Carbone would sit out there, on summer evenings, while his wife fed him skinless slices of apple. He'd had a stroke, and his face always seemed like it was pressed against an invisible windowpane he was trying to look out of.

Blue rain beat through the street lamps and the tufted palms.

"You coming?" Regimbal said. He stood beside Hopper, each of them holding a six of Rainier Ale, known to us, and to all boys in Seattle in the seventies, as green death.

About nine of us crossed Fifteenth, passing through the screen of tall black firs bordering Volunteer Park, which we called Ball-and-Queer, and headed up the sloping hill toward the art museum. We huddled under cover of the sagging bows of a blue spruce, rain dripping off the tips, outside the circle of packed dirt we sat on, and watched for the queers. A chunk of hash made the rounds in a pipe carved of bone. We all greazed on the junk me and Regimbal had bought with the food stamps. North and west of us a wide field spread out fairly flat until it dropped down a steep hill behind some trees. Beyond those trees the buoyant light of the city rose, warm and yellow. I took a sip of the warm beer and watched the horizon. The fags were like wildlife to me, wary animals that only came out at night, and hunters, too, looking for prey. I had the idea they were fags out of loneliness. That is, they came here to the park, at night, in the dark and the rain, with flash-lights, to find something a person should be able to find in an easier place, a warmer and drier and better place.

"I got attacked one night," Riles said.

I addressed his nose. "Where?"

"Down by the reservoir."

"How many?" Regimbal said. He was smoking one of Hopper's cigarettes, letting it bob from his lips. We had stopped shaving at the same time, thinking to have a race. We were like those five-and-dime toys with a magnet and a pile of metal shavings and a picture of Bluto. Regimbal, it turned out, didn't have a mustache. He had a section of goatee.

"I don't know," Riles said. "Six, seven."

We all stared at the horizon. The queers would wan-der among the trees, using flashlights to signal each other, white beams cutting through grainy, rain-slashed dark. They had a code of their own that was impossible to crack.

"They're taking over," Regimbal said.

"There's a light!" Hopper stood up. "See?"

I'd missed it. And then I saw it, two quick flashes from the right, followed by a long steady answer from the left. Hopper lifted a chunk of log and handed it to Regimbal.

"They're all over there," he said, aiming Regimbal's head. "You see? Who throws better, you or John?"

"Me," Regimbal said, although that wasn't the truth.

"Okay," Hopper said.

Regimbal tucked the log under his arm. The rain cut in a sharp slant against us as we headed out into the open field. Each of us had a beer. Green death was only available at the state liquor store, and was greatly prized for its potency. They sold it from stacked cases, always warm, which made it a decent drink for cold nights outdoors.

"I gotta piss," I said.

I took a leak in the middle of the field. My dink was still wet and sticky from Finklebien. I watched the line of trees. Some summer nights the fags flashed in the dark like fireflies. I had only begun to notice them recently, within the last year, although I assume they existed before that. I zipped up. Where I'd been holding myself, my hand had blood on it.

"Shit," I said. The blood was rust-colored.

"What?" Regimbal said. "Let me see."

"Forget it, man, get away!"

I started walking and noticed that from all the beer I'd drunk the whole world bounced.

"So we're just gonna throw that log at them?" I said.

"I hope I hit one," Regimbal said.

"Don't, man. Just get 'em to chase us."

"You chickenshit?"

I seemed to be seeing everything through water. The rain hummed in my ears. I thought I heard someone calling my name. I looked around.

"What?"

"Did you hear that?" I looked behind us. I suddenly felt awkward beside Regimbal. My body ached with awareness; I felt squeezed by silence.

The field was sloppy, pocked with puddles, and Regimbal stomped in one, spraying me with mud. I tripped him and we fell, we wrestled, rolling in the grass and mud and rain. We were boys, right, and instead of talking about what we were doing, against the silence, we banged into each other an awful lot, and this, in its own way, was a kind of discussion we were having, a debate. Afterward, muddy and wet, with grass in my hair, I felt better, easier, calmed down.

"There goes another," Regimbal said.

Two lights exchanged signals and started moving toward each other. Other lights began to flash.

"D'you find Finklebien?"

"Yeah, she was there."

"She was the only girl, you dick-for." Regimbal stopped. "D'you bang her?"

It was instinctual in me to say no, although I had the impression bragging was the more expected response. But the blood gave me a confused feeling, like I'd hurt Diane.

"Let's not do this," I said, only meaning to test it out,

see how it sounded. The rain soaked my jeans and I was cold to the bone.

"You can split if you want," Regimbal said.

When we were close enough, Regimbal swung around and around, like a discus thrower, and pitched the log into the bushes. We waited. All of a sudden the lights in the trees went nuts, came to life, flashing everywhere, sharp wavering beams searching the dark, and then, as if the lights were threads tied to us, all of them, from every angle, focused their aim our way. We were blinded. We turned and ran. Behind me I could see men with flashlights chasing after us. I raced by Regimbal, who slipped and fell in the mud. I had decided I was just going to run away, not back to Hopper and Riles and all the other crouched and waiting boys, but out of the park, into the streets, into the neighborhood. I imagined running by our house with all the fags following after me. I'd race up Fourteenth, then over to Prospect, then slip in behind Thompson's and hide in their compost pile or, if the fags were still there, I'd cut out over the fence, hit our alley, ditch through our gate, and go like mad up the tree.

At the edge of the park I turned. Not one fag had followed me. Across the dark field, I saw a mad scramble, lights twisting all over, aimlessly zipping into the sky, pointing at the ground, whizzing back and forth. Regimbal had fallen and the fags had caught him. He was screaming. Hopper and the gang charged across the field, a ragtag army of drunks, and pretty soon they were all mixed up with the fags. By the hammer swing of one light I could tell someone was getting clubbed on the head. Other flashlights lay on the ground. I hurried back. I jumped on the top of the scrum, a grunting, laughing, crying, squealing knot of legs and arms and heads, and pulled the hair of somebody who turned out to be one of our guys, one of the greasers from Renton. Regimbal was wailing down on the bottom of the pile. "I can't breathe," he screamed. "I can't fucking breathe!" I slugged somebody, I don't know who, and then somebody else slugged me in the ear, and then I got kicked repeatedly in the ass and ribs. When I got to Regimbal, I yanked him up, and he tore off. Suddenly there seemed to be no point, like a game played without a ball. Everybody ran. Everybody, those guys, the fags, me, we all ran off in different directions.

I ran up and down the streets of my neighborhood in the rain, for maybe an hour, looking for everyone. I walked as far south as Madison, the beginning of the CD, the black neighborhood, where a curious house stood on the corner, the outside walls covered with toilet seats. They gleamed beautifully in the rain, like a shipwrecked lavatory. I kept running, sometimes walking. I followed all the routes in our neighborhood, the ones we took, the places we went, me and Regimbal. Every route led to an abandoned house, or a secret tree, or a place to smoke a cigarette, or to get drunk or high. In our rambles me and Regimbal had mapped out our own city as if we were explorers in an untraveled land, although I'm aware now that other cities, more real — more lasting — than ours, ran parallel to it, skewed to it, hovered above and sat below it. There was the city where people sat down to eat dinner together, the city where men wore starched shirts and paid bills, the city where kids went to school with sandwiches wrapped in waxed paper and an apple their mothers buffed on an apron. But now it felt to me like I didn't know how to get to that city. I gave up finding anybody, and walked in the rain, watching people come home, mount their steps, and pinwheel rain from their umbrellas. I circled the streets until everything was quiet and through the windows I could see that the last lights had been put out and all the doors locked.

Somebody had put a pillow in the backseat of my dad's car, along with the blanket, but I decided it wouldn't hurt to take a shower and sleep in my own bed. I cut through the gate and started up the tree.

My window was boarded up. So was Regimbal's.

I climbed down the tree and went in through the front door. My mom and dad were sitting in the living room. Mom wore a plain sacklike dress, an afghan draped over her shoulders, yellow socks bunched at her ankles. She had just taken off her glasses, for the two red dots were still imprinted on her nose.

"How was the dance?" she asked.

"Oh," I said, but my clothes were drenched, and my hands and face were muddy, and I had grass in my hair, and my head smelled like beer, and I'd been slugged in the ear, and on top of all this my drunk was starting to come back on me, and on top of that I was just noticing my shirt was ripped, and I wasn't sure the idea of a dance was plausible at this point.

She looked at my dad, and he, I think, winked.

My dad said, "Why don't you go upstairs, dear. Leave us be."

"I am tired," she said. She kissed me. She was smiling like some kind of simple, trusting child when she said, "Good night, sweetheart."

"All the girls want to do is kiss and slow dance," I said.

When she looked at me, I could see her face squinch and cloud with confusion.

"It's late," she said. "Good night."

When she was gone, my dad said, "Let's step out back on the porch."

"You gonna hit me?"

"Now, have I ever hit you before?"

"Yeah," I said.

"Well, I guess you don't forget," he said. "You're getting too old for that, I'd say."

We stomped through the kitchen. Dad paused at the fridge and pulled out two Olys.

Outside, we sat on milk crates and watched the rain fall, pinging on our old washing machine. My dad lit a cigarette, and inhaled with great satisfaction. He was only allowed to smoke outside the house. The porch was his territory. He kept a coffee can out there for the butts, and a transistor radio for listening to broadcasts of "The Make-Believe Ballroom."

"I guess there wasn't any dance tonight," my dad said, popping open a beer and passing it to me. I was slow to take it. "That'll be me and your secret."

He cracked his beer and guzzled it in such a way that

would've put to shame any of the boys over at Carbone's. At dinner he didn't drink with nearly as much gusto.

"There was a party," I said, sipping my beer.

"Your sister apologized, by the way."

"All right."

"A party, huh? That's good," he said. "I used to love to party."

"You did?"

"Sure." He put his hand on my knee, gently flexing his fingers. I was still breathing hard. "I met your mother at a party."

"No!" I said.

"What? Why not?"

"Are you telling me the truth?"

"What the hell's wrong with you, boy? You don't believe me? You don't think I could party in my day?"

I was incredulous. I looked at him. "Was she the only girl there, at the party?"

"She was the only one I had eyes for," he said.

My palms were sweating. I wasn't sure what to do with this new information.

"Did she want to go for coffee afterwards?"

"How would I remember?"

"Well —" I felt panicked. "You don't remember if she wanted to go to IHOP after —"

"I don't think they had IHOP back then."

"How could you forget?" I wanted to know.

I felt the tide of me surging pointlessly against the breakwater of decency he'd made of his life. I got panicky, breathless. I saw myself running around the neighborhood, winded and huffing, and how I felt, nowhere near happy, but — running so that my lungs were full, as if the thrill itself had blown them up like bellows, and my heart thumped to bursting, my legs ached, my stomach pumped and sucked cool wet air — running so that the blood pounded in my ears and, even now, sitting out back and sharing a beer with my dad, I could still hear myself, hear me being alive.

JACINTA

THEY WERE MARRIED in a small white church upon a hill — that was true, a fact, but it was also a phrase Dorothy often repeated to herself, a phrase that gave her a sense of fairy-tale beginnings. The church was in LaConner, Washington. Below the hill, in all directions, low fields filled with tulips, a sea of red and yellow and purple flowers washed in waves by the coastal wind. Dorothy had timed the date of their wedding to coincide with the first blossoming of the tulips, a quilt of color stitched together by a network of dikes that held the emerald water of the Skagit River in check. Dorothy wore a simple white dress with a sweetheart neckline and an illusion veil fastened over her eyes by a coronet of pearls and intricately woven baby's breath. She felt herself hover, weightless as a high, white cloud, as she swept down the aisle on the arm of her father — he was a PR man for Weyerhaeuser, and it was through him, at a Logging Days Festival in Raymond, that she'd met Bill. They said the traditional vows, straight from the Catholic ceremony. A quiet, plain-spoken man, Bill must have found the cadence of the ceremonial language frilly and ornate, unfamiliar. He seemed almost embarrassed by the language, and there was something tentative, unsure, in his delivery. This didn't worry Dorothy, although she'd just found out she was pregnant. Bill didn't know he was a father when he said, "I do."

She told him on the way down old Highway 99. When he didn't respond immediately, Dorothy cracked her window and let the air blow her veil back: it lifted from her face, fluttering through the cab.

"Say something," she said.

Bill lifted a hand from the steering wheel and gestured helplessly — that hand worked like a conductor's baton, a silent thing whose smallest movements orchestrated emotion, and Dorothy often misread him.

"Are you disappointed?" she asked.

"No," Bill said. "Not at all."

"Her name's Jacinta."

"Who?"

Dorothy patted her stomach. "The baby."

"It might be a boy," Bill said.

"I don't feel that it is," Dorothy said. "I have a sense."

"Jacinta." Bill rolled the word over in his mouth.

"It's a stone," Dorothy said. "Also a flower, the hyacinth."

It all had happened so quickly: she was married, she was pregnant. Only yesterday, it seemed, she was meeting Bill in Raymond. That was a year ago September and the summer light was sweet and lingering. Across the field there was a refreshment stand where the Kiwanis was selling blue slushes and corn dogs on sticks and fat wedges of watermelon. Bill and Dorothy were wandering away,

out toward the edge of the fairgrounds, past the big billowing striped tents and the rickety Ferris wheel, past the
straw-and-dung smell of the paddock, out to where Bill's
truck was parked in the gravel lot. Night was coming and
the arc lights above pearled the darkening sky with blue
halos and her father's voice was floating over the public
address, faint and sad, so far away. She was slouching
down in the truck and Bill was talking. He was chewing
gum and his jaw tensed. He was rolling the sleeves of his
flannel shirt into tight doughnuts around his upper arms.
Soon the distant lights were shutting off and people were
wandering into the lot. She was closing her eyes and leaning forward in the cab, offering her lips to the dark.

Afterward, she'd found her father in the front seat
of his car with a can of Oly and a cigarette, the long, dead
ash curling down. When she opened the door, it fell into
his lap. They sat silently in the empty lot and Dorothy
listened to a man laughing happily and to the ring of coins
falling as someone counted change. Her father remained
silent and withdrawn all the way back to Annie Wright,
a girl's prep school in Tacoma. The school had a certain
cachet in her mother's mind because Mary McCarthy had
spent some time there; her mother hoped Dorothy would
pursue Mary McCarthy one step further and attend Vas-
sar. Her mother worshipped Culture and things "back
East" and gave everyone the impression that she was suffering some kind of terrible exile. In the circular drive,
her father shifted into park and let the car idle. He sipped
his beer and in the dim light his lips stood out, moist and
red in a face otherwise old and gray. Dorothy could see

the dark silhouettes of her dormmates drifting across the curtained windows.

"You know, dear," her father said. "I don't love your mother." He finished his beer and then pried two triangular holes in the top of another. "Isn't that a hell of a thing?"

She had waited for an explanation, but there was none.

All that year Bill left work early on Fridays and drove north from Hood River to visit Dorothy in Tacoma. There was a small state park on the tip of Vashon Island where he pitched a tent and slept after he'd returned Dorothy to the dorm just in time to make her midnight curfew. In his hair and the rough wool of his Pendleton shirts was always the smell of alder smoke and salt water. Her friends knew of the affair and envied Dorothy: the thought of a man camped out on a wooded island across the water struck them as deeply, incredibly romantic. They all had the idea, at Annie Wright, that they'd been locked away in a tower to languish unloved forever.

Bill and Dorothy moved to a small white house at the end of a dusty access road that wound through an apple orchard owned by Homer Jorgenson, a man Bill had known all his life. Homer had built the house for his parents, built it himself during the war, requisitioning the wood with a lie — telling the government he needed the lumber to re-build a barn blown over by a storm that had howled up the Columbia Gorge that spring. Homer — who'd never married — had given Bill a job as an overseer, running the orchard. Homer was sixty years old, an angular man who looked as though he'd been carved into his current hard shape by a constant wind, by slow erosion, by long resistance; when he stood still, his body leaned forward slightly, like a scrub pine perched on a sea cliff. His solitary life had not made him fussy, the way some men get. He'd lived on the same eight hundred acres of apple orchard all his life and so had his father and grandfather before him, and there was something in that continuity that sat contentedly in Homer's bones; deep down he knew exactly what he had to do — laying out and lighting smudge pots all night to ward off a sudden frost, tracking and killing a cougar that had come down from the mountains and attacked the few head of cattle he kept.

As a wedding gift, Homer had fixed up the little house: he'd rolled a fresh coat of thick white paint over the interior walls, he'd installed a new gas stove and reglazed the front windows and cleared the chimney of a bird's nest. When Bill and Dorothy entered their new home for the first time, the nest, as neatly woven as a wicker basket, sat alone on the dinner table, and in the hollowed center were two keys twisted together by a blue ribbon: one key worked the front door and the other opened the gun cabinet. In the cabinet, they'd found a bottle of champagne floating in a bucket of lukewarm water. It was a nice gesture, they'd just arrived late. Dorothy loved the little house, but something about it felt boxy and austere, the idea of a man who lived alone. She immediately set about cluttering the walls with pictures and mirrors and, in the kitchen window, she arranged her collection of Japanese fishing floats, globes of colored glass used to buoy drift nets. For a few hours every day, late in the afternoon, when the sun slanted over Mount Hood in a fan of cloud-broken light, "God's light" as it was called, the floats lifted the plain white room out of itself, into another realm, giving it the bright, swimming color of a church awash with the blues and reds and greens of stained glass windows.

Early one morning, not long after they'd settled in, Bill was sitting on the porch with a cup of black coffee and his Freedom Arms 454, a sidearm with enough stopping power to drop a bear at thirty yards. Dorothy heard the report in her dreams as Bill, between sips of steaming coffee, shot a yearling not twenty feet from their doorstep. He'd winched the doe upside down from the branch of the single apple tree in their yard and was gutting it when she came out onto the porch. Close by the trees were black and shadowy but far off the leaves shimmered a dewy silver in the sunlight. The apples were still green on the branch. Bill slit the doe's throat and the blood spilled to the ground as if from a spigot. The knife he used shone in the morning sun, a knife, it seemed to Dorothy, from some kind of ancient lore — the silver blade, a shaft of light as Bill plunged it hilt-deep into the doe's dark belly and opened the interior to the sun, pulling the gut wide open and allowing the light to pour in as if that were his only intention all along. Then the entrails fell out, hot and steaming, on the wet, green grass.

Homer had heard the shot echo and walked up through the trees from his place. He looked at the doe and the bloody grass and then scratched his head, running his fingers through his thick white hair. Dorothy had noticed about Homer that he always combed his hair, that it always smelled of some pomade and stood stiffly and neatly in place, no matter what hour of the day. It suggested, to Dorothy, a childhood habit. She imagined that his bed was made each morning, too.

"Young," Homer said.

"Year or more," Bill said. Sunlight caught the glistening fat and for an instant the doe looked like tallow hanging from the tree, a burning candle twisting gently in the wind.

Bill wrapped the soft heart in a scrap of newspaper.

"Like to clear the dragline ditch out front," Homer said. "Drainage is bad."

"Be right on it," Bill said. "Soon as I'm done here."

Dorothy's breasts and the swelling curve of her belly showed through her thin, gauzy robe. She saw Homer staring, and the exposure gave her a pleasant sensation. Bill looked, too. A light wind blew, and in the quiet, for a moment, it was as if her presence were somehow at issue. Dorothy crossed her arms in front of her, almost to break the spell and help the men resume their discussion. Homer looked across the orchard in the direction of Mount Hood, a white cone of snow carved like a cameo against the clearing blue sky.

Bill said, "How about some coffee?"

When Dorothy ducked inside, Homer said, "This wasn't really necessary."

Bill squinted. "It was there. Snuck up on me."

"That's no reason."

"Well," Bill said. "It's done."

Dorothy came out of the house with two cups. Her

feet were bare and the blades of grass, tender spring growth, soft and damp, felt pleasant against her skin. She had lately been feeling bloated and dull, a heavy, waddling thing, but the grass brushing beneath her feet momentarily relieved her of that, and lifted her spirits.

"Your husband here's getting a nesting urge. Some kind of sympathetic deal. Happens to men."

Bill said, "This'll come in handy when you're laid up, Dot."

"Are you promising to cook?" Dorothy asked.

He wiped his hands on his trousers. "I don't know that I'm saying that."

"I'll cook," Homer said. A lifelong bachelor, he'd acquired a kind of domestic felicity that made him, at times, seem feminine. Dorothy had borrowed cups of sugar and flour from Homer and traded recipes with him, walking back and forth along the worn dirt path between the two houses; he didn't seem at all out of place when he wrapped the strings of an apron around his waist and stood before a kitchen stove crowded with simmering pots, a smudge of baking soda on his forehead. But it was more than this, more than a man with a whisk in his hand, more than a man bent over the counter to pick a piece of shell from a cup of egg whites; alone for so long, he had taken up the role because there was no one to assign it to.

"I make a good venison stew," he said. "We can freeze up a batch."

"That'd be nice," Dorothy said.

"I'd've rather married you," Bill said, "had I known your secret talents."

"What's that supposed to mean?" Dorothy asked.

Bill said, "Hell, I don't know."

The doe turned a slow circle, winding and unwinding in the wind.

"There's more coffee on, you want it," Dorothy said.

When she walked away, she felt the men watching her; she was intensely aware of how wide she'd gotten, how heavy and overripe. Their scrutiny made each footstep awkward and calculated; she thought she might stumble. She wanted to feel weightless and walked immediately to the back of the house, where she began filling the claw-footed tub. With the water running, she went back to the kitchen for a cup of tea. A trail of blood marked her path, perfect red prints of her big toe and the wide flat pad of her foot, like a strange animal, moving across the linoleum, the pine planks, the carpet, the tiles in the bathroom. The bright oxygenated blood had seeped through the wet grass. She grabbed a washcloth from the kitchen sink, scrubbed the stains away as best she could, and when the tub was full, she lowered herself into the water, briefly felt buoyant and free of burden, and then, awkwardly, she reached forward and washed her feet.

Jacinta was born in August and she died a year later without ever speaking a word. She had learned to walk, she had learned to climb the couch and scale the kitchen chairs, with Bill teaching her, praising her handholds, urging her on, taking delight in her wordless joy. A few days after her first birthday she drowned in a shallow tin trough full of rainwater. Early in the afternoon, she climbed over the lip of the trough and when Bill found her, she was floating facedown, her short blond hair curling away from her head like weeds in the clear water. Dorothy was frosting an apple spice cake when Bill ran across the yard holding Jacinta in his arms like a bundle of dripping rags. He set her on the dining table and unzipped her pink jumpsuit. He bent down. He plugged her nose and placed his mouth over hers and breathed into her. Jacinta's stomach inflated with every entering breath and then flattened again. A slight sound of exhaling, a secret whisper could be heard in the quiet room as Bill's breath flowed back out through her lifeless mouth. He rose up and drew breath, then went back down, as if to place a kiss on her lips. Festoons of limp party streamers twirled lazily above Bill, streamers from several days ago and a small celebration they'd had. Dorothy gripped the back of Bill's shirt as he tried to breathe life into Jacinta. He began pounding his fist against her baby's heart. A gurgle of water spilled from her lips. Dorothy called Homer. Homer called for an ambulance. Bill kept at it for half an hour, breathing, pounding, pumping her stomach to clear her windpipe, when at last the ambulance arrived from town. Even then, Bill wouldn't stop. Finally, Homer put a hand on his shoulder, then pulled hard. Bill looked up. He seemed surprised to see anyone else standing there.

"There's nothing you can do," Homer said. "She's dead."

Bill glanced back at Jacinta, and for a moment he seemed like a brave man, the kind of man who would walk away and never look back again, and then he looked directly at Dorothy.

"Who the hell are you staring at?" he said. His hands were trembling, and he clutched the seams of his pant legs to calm them.

Dorothy went out the door, shocked into silence. It had rained hard the night before, but now the sun was out and a strong steady wind blew through the trees. Shadows shifted like living things on the grass. With a house in the middle of an orchard, it was difficult to know where the yard ended and the world began — rows and rows of apple trees angled away into a shimmering, sunlit infinity. She stopped at the trough. It was no bigger than a washtub. A few green leaves floated on the surface, and when she looked in, Dorothy saw her face, reflected on the still surface and framed in white clouds. She believed then — or later, maybe — that Jacinta had seen her own reflection floating on the surface, too, a round face drifting with the mirrored blue and white of the sky, and that she had tried to follow her image up into that heaven, and instead went down into the darkness, where she drowned. Dorothy walked to the barn and found an awl. She punched a single small hole in the trough, a hole the size of a star. She watched the blue sky and the white shifting clouds pour out onto the lawn. The water drained slowly. She bent down and cupped her hand under the tiny flow and drank from the water as it dribbled away between her fingers. She stayed until the trough was empty.

The ambulance had pulled away on the road toward town, moving slowly, its lights off. Dorothy returned to the house. Homer leaned against the kitchen counter, his hands folded. Bill sat on the couch, gazing at the white wall in front of him. He had not spoken since the paramedic lifted Jacinta's perfect and lifeless form from a puddle of water on the table and carried her, still dripping, to the ambulance.

"If it hadn't rained," Dorothy said.

"It did rain," Bill said. His voice was calm. "It rained all fucking night."

Dorothy stuck a leftover birthday candle in the center of the cake and held a match to the wick. The tiny flame rose around the black wick in the shape of two hands folded in prayer. She felt pitiful. "God," she said. Bill looked up at her as if he were blind and had only heard a slight movement in the corner of the room. Dorothy would have preferred anger, outrage, anything but this calm that came from some heartless place Bill had discovered in himself.

"Let's sing," Dorothy said. The kitchen was flooded with a wash of red and blue and green light from the floats lined along the sill. "Okay, we don't have to sing. Maybe singing's not a good idea." She started to cry. "I don't know why not, though."

Bill left the house, kicking the screen door off its hinge. Homer held Dorothy by the shoulders, then hugged her. The candle still burned in the cake.

Homer rocked Dorothy in his arms, and she could feel the spare, necessary arrangement of him — the bone, the muscle, the rough skin where his face scraped against her temple. She saw over his shoulder the alarm clock, and the time blinked off and on, a green insult. A clean wind pushed at the curtains, and she could smell Scotch broom in the air. She heard a train whistle echoing in the

Gorge. A dog barked, and then there was a long silence. Dorothy listened. It was quiet for a long time, but she imagined new sounds already out there, moving toward her, crossing that wide space.

"That candle's going to go out," Homer said.

He wet his fingers with spittle and pinched the flame. He eased Dorothy down on the couch and then went to work in the kitchen. He started two new potatoes in a pan of boiling water and chopped fresh parsley and shaved slivers of garlic. He set two stick matches in his mouth and sliced open an onion. "Keeps the tears away," he said, chewing on the matchsticks. He fried a chunk of bacon and dipped two small rainbow trout in the fat and rolled them in cornmeal and cooked them quickly in an iron skillet alive with the sizzle of grease.

"You want to talk, go ahead," Homer said. "I'm listening."

The garlic and onion went with a thick pad of butter into another pan and when they were ready Homer cut up the potatoes and put them in.

Dorothy absently traced the molded ear of Jacinta's favorite doll — one that wept when you filled a little reservoir in its head with water. Her daughter was gone, but here was the dumb doll, here was the kitchen sink with the brown splotch of mineral stain, here was the wide plank floor of soft pine that still had the same pocked surface it had yesterday, and the day before, making it a map of rearranged sofas and chairs, of the places people had sat and talked and eaten and loved and fought in the forty years since the house was built.

Homer set a plate in front of Dorothy. He put a white paper napkin on her lap and a fork in her hand. He said, "Eat."

"What about Bill?" she asked.

"Just eat. He'll come back."

Dorothy ate; it was enough to move her mouth over something solid.

Late that night, Dorothy went into the barn. She unhooked a wool blanket from a nail on the wall and sat beside Bill. He was curled up. A bottle of vodka lay tipped over and empty at his side. His hair was matted with dirt and straw and white molted feathers, and from his mouth, pressed against the ground, a dark drool stain spread in the dirt. He kicked the hard-packed earth with the toe of his boots as if he were trying to prod an answer from it. Dorothy bent down to him and turned his face. His nose was bleeding. His lips were caked with crumbs of dirt. She brushed them clean and kissed them. His breath was a damp, sour wind rising from within the cavern of his mouth.

In the weeks following the funeral, Dorothy began attending daily Mass. She wasn't so much religious as spiritual, and with the church, she shopped her way through the dogma, tossing out what she considered old and rotten, keeping what was ripe and beautiful. She didn't need rules written in stone; she was there for the slant of light through the lofty row of windows, the blue hush of votive candles in the quiet moments before the first mournful intonations of the Latin High Mass began — there was something about a dead tongue speaking, that she loved, and the words, loosed from the weight of meaning, floated free, a music in which she could drift forever.

Bill mended section fences, roofed the barn, and drank in the early evenings with the migrants. He'd start with them in the afternoon and come home and continue drinking in his chair, balancing his glass on the arm and watching Dorothy, silently, as she cooked dinner. He kept his liquor in the unlocked gun cabinet and when he was finished for the night he returned his glass and the spoon he used as a swizzle, both unwashed, to the shelf, next to his bottle. Once, when Dorothy had washed the glass and spoon, Bill blew up at her, angry in the calm way that had become his manner — he squeezed her arm so tightly that a bruise in the shape of his thumbprint showed purple and yellow just below her shoulder. His eyes held some kind of unfocused enormity, but all he said was, "Don't. Don't. Don't." Now, when he watched her work over the stove, his blank eyes bearing down, Dorothy was afraid; and in her fear, she became forgetful, letting things burn to black or boil limply in the pan until the water was nearly gone.

Upstairs, in bed, with a wind whistling through the chinking in the walls, or the windows rattling, or the hazy light of town hovering above the trees, or a sliver of gold moon slipped into a corner pane, or the slow red blinking of a jet from Portland passing up and out of her view, Dorothy would lie still, alert. She was uncomfortably aware of her body, keeping it frozen in a single position until, heavy and numb, time itself seemed to stop. Nightly, for several weeks, Bill took her — no kisses, no real touching, no tentative exploration, he'd turn her over and enter her with a quick stab from behind and jerk hastily above her buttocks and, when done, withdraw immediately and fall asleep. Dorothy would remain awake. She began spending most nights awake on a wicker love seat, beneath the window. She'd look at her husband, buried in the quilt. He'd be smiling, as if there'd been a joke; he often smiled in his sleep, in the silent hours when she watched. Toward dawn, she'd fall asleep, and there would be dreams, dreams of sun and sand and the shadow of something, a fox or coyote, but in the morning, there was always nothing.

One morning she stayed after Mass to visit with the parish priest, Father McGill. Grains of rice from a wedding had settled into the black gummy tar that lined the seams of the sidewalk, and Dorothy stood outside, after the blessing, as the parishioners filed away, each placing a hand still wet with holy water in Father's pink palm; there were always a few men who attended daily Mass, but only, it seemed, out of some lack of vigor — jobless, retired, crippled, lonely. Mostly, it was a congregation of women who wore old shabby clothes that dated from the last days of their happiness, women who wore black and mourned losses that were lost, irrevocably, years ago. As Dorothy watched them, she worried about becoming one of those crazed, wounded women who always wore hats in the old manner and arrived before Mass to kneel in a long wooden pew and pray solemnly, muttering aloud, with a bowed head, alone in their lunatic sorrow.

When they were by themselves, Dorothy said, "Can I talk with you, Father?"

"Of course," he said.

He touched her elbow and guided her back into the church, into the cool, dark air, and together they walked up the aisle, genuflecting before the altar. To Dorothy, it seemed strange to do this when no one was around, to kneel and cross herself in the empty church, like a kind of mime show. Father McGill led her across the sanctuary, through a door; he offered her a card chair, and they sat together in the sacristy.

"Would you like to make a confession?" Father asked.

"No," Dorothy said, "that's not why I've come. I'm not here about me."

She knew the church from her seat in the nave and had never stood in the sanctuary and certainly had never entered the vestry, this back room where the priest slipped on his soutane and knotted tight his cincture. She looked around. A frayed veronica hung from the wall, a replica, obviously — it was from one of the stations of the cross, but Dorothy couldn't remember which. Cases of novitiate wine were stacked in a corner. A plastic bag lay on the counter — white wafers with a blue twist tie pinching the neck of the sack closed.

Father McGill waited patiently.

"You know our daughter died," Dorothy said.

"Yes," Father said.

"Since then our marriage has been difficult."

She knew she needed to talk about her body, needed to talk about the relationship Bill had with it; he had stopped his nightly taking of her, no longer touched her at all, but the fear she felt had not gone away.

Father fingered the tassled tip of his cincture. "How so?"

"I'm afraid that I will have to leave him." Dorothy had not considered the possibility until the words were spoken aloud. As she looked at Father McGill, the words sounded cruel and harsh, and she wanted them back immediately.

"A marriage is not a thing to abandon lightly."

"Every breath is a crisis," she said. "When he's around, I can't breathe."

"Your daughter's death has placed a terrible strain on your relationship," Father said. He looked at her benevolently. His hands were folded in his lap. "Is it possible that time itself will mend it?"

"I don't know," Dorothy said.

"She died in August, if I remember. It's now March. Eight months."

"It feels longer."

"Tragedy always does. The Mass itself is two thousand years old."

Dorothy realized she did not want to speak about this in religious terms. She wanted practical advice. She looked at Father McGill and then at the counter with the bag of wafers. Crystal cruets of wine and water rested in a silver tray. Behind Father was a door that led outside.

"I suppose you're right," Dorothy said.

"Of course," Father said. He stood and opened the door. Light poured in and lit up the green walls of the sacristy. It was an ugly, small room. Dorothy had only once in her life entered the home of a blind person, and it, too, had been painted this same unpleasant green.

"Stay with him," Father said. "He needs you."

Every morning Bill drove the rutted two-track through the orchard in an old Ford flatbed loaded with migrants and day pickers and before coming home he stopped nightly at the row of dirty white shacks and bet on the cockfights. Through the kitchen window, in the fading light of early evening, Dorothy would see the trail of bleached white dust rising from the road and know Bill was headed for the fights. El Blanco, the Mexicans called him. They'd cordoned off a patch of packed dirt with chicken wire and stakes of light gauge rebar and the men sat around the ring on old barrels and wooden boxes and car seats. The cocks fought until one of them sliced open the other's throat with tiny razor blades attached to their feet. When it grew dark, someone would pull a car or two up to the ring and turn on the headlights, and the men would sprawl on the hoods, and their drunken shouts and cries would rise in a plume of dust and echo across the orchard for Dorothy to hear.

Bill had started an affair with a young Mexican girl and told Dorothy. His confession seemed calculated to drive her away. Dorothy had visited the girl once and come away with nothing. She had not gone to threaten the girl or warn her or cause a scene. She had gone because she loved her husband with a love that had never been in question, and she wanted to know about him, about his secret life, his Mexican girl and the cockfights, and what it was, possibly, that he had found in the dusty compound of white

shacks — that world of clotheslines fluttering and alive
with hand-washed shirts and dungarees, of trikes tipped
over in the dirt, a bent front wheel turning slowly in the
wind. The girl hardly spoke English, but Dorothy got the
impression, as she listened to the mangled sentences, that
this girl had dreams of a lasting relationship with Bill;
there was a cloudy hint of covetousness in her words, a
hint of washing machines, of running cars, of a charmed
life in the house of the gringo foreman. It all sounded
proud and bitter and aggressive to Dorothy.

Later that night, when Bill got home and took up his
seat, he began to cry. He didn't make a sound. His shoulders didn't heave. His lips didn't quiver. Tears fell slowly
from his clear blue eyes, drop by drop, as though ice were
melting, and then dried on his face. He did not wipe the
tears away.

Dorothy knelt at the foot of his chair. "Bill?"

He stared past her, unmoved. Dorothy reached for
Bill's shoulder; he slapped her hand down.

"Don't touch me," he said.

"I want to talk," Dorothy said.

"Talk," he said.

"I don't want to just talk to nothing," she said. "This
can't go on."

"Sure it can," Bill said. "It can go on forever."

She went back to the stove and stirred a pot of squash.

"You're always watching me, you're always looking at
me," she said. He was looking right at her, his steady stare
bore down, but Dorothy had the impression he wasn't
listening. She continued anyway. "I'm starting to feel crazy

a lot. I don't feel like anything I do is free. Everything, every move is wrong. I'm afraid of you."

His silence belittled and dismissed her words. From the shelf above the sink, she took one of her floats, a green float with a flawed seam, a float her sister had sent her from Seattle, and pitched it at the wall behind Bill. The glass shattered and rained to the floor.

Bill sipped from his drink. "Your aim is off."

She sat up with Homer and Bill that night. When Homer came around, things were better; he drank heavily but only seemed to mellow, to grow gentle as the night wore on, sinking into himself and settling there, comfortably. When Bill ranted, dropping into his private shorthand, Homer was always careful to nod knowingly and sympathetically to Dorothy, letting her understand she was not entirely alone. She was grateful — Homer had kept Bill busy around the orchard, and when work fell slack, they went to the mountains; he got Bill involved with the Mount Hood Search and Rescue Team, and together they had climbed Mount Adams and Mount Rainier. Bill always came home calmed after one of their climbs, as if the mountain were still in him, a high peak on which he stood, looking down from that distance at the daily life he lived.

Bill and Homer talked, dreamily, of a trip to Nepal. Together, they seemed to know every mountain in the world, and when they talked, growing excited, there seemed to be a freedom in the planning of things that would never be. Himalaya, Bill said, meant the home of snow.

"Why go so far?" Dorothy asked.

Quoting Mallory, Bill said, "Because it's there."

Dorothy frowned. "That's dumb," she said.

"There's no other reason," Bill said. "You go because they're there. If they weren't there, where would you go? What if everything was flat? Where would you go then? You'd go nowhere, right, because every place would be the same."

"You're not making sense, Bill."

"Maybe not to you," he said but decided to try again. "If everything was flat and the same, you'd never have to go anywhere because nothing anywhere else would be different, you'd be like God, everywhere and fucking nowhere in particular."

"Sounds like hell," Dorothy said. She got up and fixed another drink. She realized she didn't really care what Bill said as long as he kept talking.

"That's right," Bill said.

"Me," Homer said, "I've got to go because I'm getting old. I'm on my next-to-last switchback." He smiled at his own corniness. He bit an ice cube. "You live alone, you don't notice life passing by so much."

Dorothy sat down, crossing her legs; her shorts hitched up along her thigh. She did not find it unpleasant to be exposed, to be looked at. When she met Homer's eye, he averted his face. He shifted his feet.

"Home of snow," he repeated. "A Piper Cub crashed on the summit of Mount Hood about ten years ago. It got lost in a cloud cap. Don't know what it was doing up there."

"Trying to see the summit," Dorothy offered.

"Can't see anything in a cloud," Homer said. "They crashed going about ninety, I guess. The plane flipped, and when they released their seat belts, they fell on their heads. These guys were businessmen, they had on business suits." Homer poured out two fingers of scotch. "It snowed every day for a week, no one could get to them. Five feet of snow covered the airplane, and that was their good luck. The snow kept them warm inside their buried plane. They survived."

"Thank God for snow," Bill said.

"That plane's still up there, right?"

"Yeah," Bill said. "Still." He stared into his glass.

That night was like other nights, nights when he would talk of mountains, mountains that he'd never seen but knew were out there just as men once knew the edge of the world waited beyond the horizon. Bill came alive when he talked of mountains, of climbs, of snow — especially snow: he would talk about powder snow, corn snow, rotten snow, of suncrust and windcrust and rime and hoarfrost, of firn mirror and the way slope angle and sunlight will create a brilliant sheen of glacier fire; he'd seen this once, a bright golden ribbon of fire showing a path right up the mountain to the summit; and he spoke of sun cups and fields of nieves penitentes on higher elevations, columns of snow, like nuns in a church, slanting with a slight forward bow toward the midday sun. He talked of spindrift, of cornices, of silver thaw when an inch of ice coats everything so that rocks seemed to be made of glass and trees are encased in crystal. "Nothing moves," he said. "If anything moves, it cracks. You can hear the crashing like breaking glass. Everything shatters." Time holds still in the higher elevations, he would say. "That high, that cold, things don't change. They're preserved. Even the body, when it drops to ninety degrees — two, three heartbeats a minute, that's all. You can't know if a man's alive then." Time is visible, you can see it, he would insist, as wind currents pass over the snow and leave their shape behind in the form of drifts and cornices, like waves that curl and never break.

"Snow ghosts," Homer said.

"They look like people," Bill said.

He went to the gun cabinet and poured another drink. He looked at Homer and said, "Me and her, we don't sleep together anymore."

"Please, Bill," Dorothy said.

"You want my wife." He sipped his drink. "I see you looking. I've seen you before."

Bill swallowed his drink, set the spoon in the glass, and placed the works in his cabinet.

"I'm tired," he said. "Good night."

When he'd gone upstairs, Dorothy said, "He doesn't mean it."

"You sleep together?" Homer said.

"No," Dorothy said, embarrassed. "He makes a show of driving me away, when that isn't what he means. He wants me around, to witness everything."

A while later, Dorothy said good night to Homer. He bent forward to kiss her, an awkward, dry kiss, and then instantly vanished into the stand of cedar between their homes. Dorothy went upstairs. She walked in front of Bill, crossing the path of his stare. Slowly she undressed herself. She unbuttoned her blouse and let it slough to the floor.

She let her breasts fall from the cups of her bra and then stood there, holding them. The nipples hardened under her fingers. She felt her own touch and caress travel the length of her body. She stepped out of her shorts and faced Bill.

"You didn't go with him?" he said.

She sat on the edge of the bed. After Jacinta was buried, Bill had gone through the house, removing her clothes, her toys, her crib; he'd taken down all the pictures from the walls and the snapshots pinned with magnets to the fridge; he'd torn them up in a monstrous frenzy. There had been one large, framed studio portrait of Jacinta on the wall above Dorothy's dresser; it was a portrait that Dorothy remembered from long lazy afternoon naps when she and Jacinta would lie in the bed, and a shaft of light, solid with drifting dust, would cut through the window; when Bill destroyed the picture, a clean, white space remained on the wall, and that blank so unnerved Dorothy that she had taken a bucket and sponge and scrubbed the entire surface. Still, now, it seemed to float there for a moment. She dismissed the apparition as an optical trick.

Dorothy had purchased an open bus ticket to Seattle, where her sister lived, and twice in the past month she'd gone to the station. It was a small dingy station, little more than a ticket window and a wooden bench with an ashtray at one end, full of gum wrappers and cigarette butts and chewed toothpicks; behind the bench was a row of rental lockers. She had folded her ticket and slipped it into a small travel bag she kept stowed in one of the lockers. At certain moments in her day, she would think of the depot, of her locker and her ticket to Seattle, but in the two times she'd gone to town, the reality of the dingy station frightened her away.

The second time she stood outside the door, frozen. Inside, a soldier sat slumped on the bench, his green duffle on the floor, a pair of headphones in his ears; a little girl with stringy blond hair fingered the coin slot of the candy machine, looking for change; her mother stood by a large window that fronted the street, looking out, her face freckled by the light pouring through the dirty pane. At her feet rested two suitcases, a naked doll, and a hair dryer.

Dorothy walked away from the station, through town. Daylilies bloomed along the borders of driveways and sidewalks, in little islands on the lawns. The better houses had clipped, square hedges. A good, clearing breeze tossed the chestnut trees, shaking the burred fruit into the street, scratching dryly in the gutters. Children were getting out of school now and running in ragged circles, their coats flapping, their hands waving hectic finger-paint pictures of bunnies and Easter eggs. Mothers, in pairs, strolled along behind. Dorothy slipped past them with her head down.

She walked toward the park above town. Now and then, winded, she looked over her shoulder, taking in more and more of the view as she climbed. Lights came on slowly in the shops and bars. The lowering sun hit Mount Hood on its western slope, and a shadow spread, cold and blue, over the eastern face. In a sandbox down the hill, some children played tag, spun, dipped, fell, shouted, trying to catch one another. A mother shouted for them to come home. A gang of older kids had set a bonfire in one of the grates. They drank beer and joked, their voices echoing crisply in the cold. The clear evening air had a nip to it; if it got cold enough tonight, Bill and Homer would fill the smudge pots with oil, and the fires would smolder and burn in the orchards, glowing orange and blue in the hills that sloped to the Gorge, keeping the early buds alive.

A train whistled in the Gorge, across the Washington side of the river. At this distance, the river looked still; the Columbia was wide, more like a lake than a river flowing toward the Pacific. A yellow beacon flashed in the shipping lane, marking a safe depth for the boats from Japan, Venezuela, Greece. Voices from town carried up to the park. Dorothy heard a thick ring of keys jangling against a lock. A stoplight changed, green. A containership edged out into the lane, its bulky black hull visible only in outline now, a darker thing than the night. The decks were lit, the men moving around, small and shadowy, but it was the hull Dorothy watched, down below, black, cutting the water. Hood River wasn't a port exactly, but it was only forty miles through the Gorge to Astoria, and then there was open sea, the Pacific, just over the rough Columbia Bar.

When she returned home that night, she heard Bill's voice upstairs. She knew instantly what was going on, but it was too late for betrayal, too late for hurt, too late for scenes. She set her purse on the counter and slipped off her coat. She tied an apron around her waist and inspected the fridge; two thick steaks thawed in a metal pan, the white butcher paper stained with pink juice. She took them out, placed them on the slotted broiler pan, and set the temperature. She could hear the soft pad of bare feet upstairs, the toilet flushing, the water washing down through the pipes. She understood vaguely that she was broken and could offer no resistance, that her life was a dream, and that whatever happened was perfectly all right. She stabbed the steaks with a fork and salted them and slipped them in the oven, setting the timer on the stove.

Bill came downstairs. "You were gone."

"Town," she said.

He sat at the table. She placed a fork and knife and napkin in front of him.

"She can't stay up there all night," Dorothy said.

"No, I guess not." Bill was turning shy, soft; it was an old comic routine, a bedroom farce, and the familiarity drained him, momentarily, of his ferocity.

"Yolanda," he called upstairs.

She came down. She'd combed her hair, and in the hall light, it shone raven and dark, almost blue. She hesitated in the kitchen, looking around, and then touched Bill's shoulder on the way out.

Dorothy served dinner. She ate in silence, cutting the meat into small, precise pieces, listening to the tines of her fork scrape the plate, to the serrated edge of the knife saw the steak, watching the shadow of Bill's hand rise and fall across the table. When they had finished, she cleared their plates and began to clean up. Bill fixed a drink and hovered behind her, leaning against the counter. He sipped from his glass and the ice clinked and Dorothy felt the sound at the base of her neck. It traveled down her spine.

"What were you doing in town?"

A fleck of pepper, she noticed, floated in the rinse water. She pinched it out with her finger.

"You done talking forever?"

She worked a washrag over a fork, even though it was already clean.

"Funny," Bill said. But he didn't say what he found funny.

Dorothy had the vague impression that if she kept washing, if she kept reaching into the sink and turning on the faucet and scrubbing the knives and forks, then Bill would recognize her, he would see in her something old and familiar, and she would be saved.

"What the hell," Bill said. He bit down on an ice cube. It cracked loudly in his open mouth.

She imagined herself mixing batters, spooning blueberries in muffin tins, baking breads and rolls, roasting a chicken, a stew simmering on the stove. She imagined lining the cupboards with fresh paper and ironing Bill's good shirts and fanning magazines out across the coffee table. She imagined running the vacuum, picking up shirt pins, paper clips, buttons, bending over to pocket a penny, which, after all, might be the lucky one.

She lifted a plate from the sink and then braced herself. She felt his anger coming before it arrived, a sudden stillness. His fist landed on the side of her face, near the eye. The plate sank back through the suds, into the water. She turned from the force of the blow. His fist was still clenched, and he raised it to his mouth, biting into a whitened knuckle. He dropped his hands to his sides and began to shudder convulsively in a pained mimicry of someone crying; there were no tears in his eyes, they were dry, drier than stone.

"Hold me," he begged.

The embrace was only the memory of an embrace, a lesson learned and repeated rote-like. He had hit her, but it was too late for them to touch. Bill sat down in his chair, and Dorothy walked out the door. Spiderwebs spread across the path, holding in their threads some of the light rain that had begun to fall. Dorothy broke through them blindly.

When Homer answered his door, immediately he asked, "What happened?" But he knew. He sat Dorothy down in an old rocking chair that had been his grandfather's. He pushed the chair back and forth and said, "You can stay here if you want."

"I'm leaving."

"I wish that wasn't so."

"I can't remember anything anymore. Nothing, you know?"

Homer disappeared into his kitchen and brought back a damp cloth. He'd slipped two ice cubes in the center, and now he held the bundle to her swelling eye.

"I wish there was some revelation," Dorothy said. "Something you could tell me about Bill that I don't already know."

"There's no excuse."

"It's not just the baby."

Dorothy had never been above the first floor of the

house, but she had been right: Homer's bed was neatly made, a thick blanket bought from the Umpquas was spread crisply over the mattress, and two pillows with bright green cases lay beneath the headboard, strangely waiting. Homer had been so long alone that Dorothy had half imagined he might have dispensed with one of the pillows, gotten rid of it as unnecessary, an extravagance, a charade. But he had two pillows, and he also had night-stands with identical shaded lamps flanking either side of the bed.

She went to the bathroom. A black comb rested on the lip of the sink. Two clean towels were stacked on top of a silver radiator. On the wall next to the bathtub hung a picture of Jacinta. Homer was holding her aloft, above his head, in the backyard beside the apple tree. That apple tree, Homer had said, was the first in the orchard, planted by his grandfather, a sapling ordered from a catalogue. Beside the picture of Jacinta was an old tintype from the days when the whole world was recorded in a mild golden hue; Homer's grandfather stood over the sapling, proudly pointing at its tiny, bare, twiglike branches. Behind him, the far background was vague, but closer in there was a clear-cut field of stumps. The shadow of the photographer crept into a corner of the picture, a dark hooded shape that gave the scene a feeling of silence.

In the bedroom, the windows were open.

"Don't cry," Homer said. "Everything's going to be fine."

He clasped her waist and bent to kiss her at the open throat of her blouse. When he folded back the fabric and ran a finger under the lacy fringe of her bra, her chest heaved in a sudden stutter; she trembled from the cold and the simple exposure. The curtains lifted. A brown-and-white feather floated across a small writing desk and sailed to the floor. Homer shut the windows, and Dorothy continued undressing. When she was naked her skin seemed incredibly white, like something long buried. Homer eased her down on the edge of the bed and asked, "Are you sure?" It wasn't really a question she could answer. Homer undressed, hanging his shirt in the closet, draping his slacks over the back of a chair. A quarter fell from the pocket and rolled in circles and wobbled to a stop beneath the bed.

Dorothy had returned home and was waiting for daybreak when the call came — a party was lost in a freak spring snowstorm that had wrapped around the western face of the mountain.

While Bill dressed upstairs, Dorothy started coffee. In a sort of ritual trance, scrubbing dishes in a slow, circular motion, she continued where she left off the night before. Islands of cold grease whitened on the plates. She ran them under the scalding water and watched the islands thaw and loosen and slide away. She wiped a rag over a plate and was aware, suddenly, that she always cleaned in a counterclockwise motion, as if cleaning were the reverse of time, an action against it. Beyond the kitchen window, a fringe of morning glory clung to the window frame; beyond that, Dorothy saw nothing but a murky gray light. Her reflection was still solid in the window, the mess of red hair, the white slope of her throat as it curved from sight. A gray bruise shut her left eye. Dorothy caught herself staring and, with a dull shock of recognition, turned away, reaching into the warm water for another dish.

As he dressed, Bill ran through the next twenty-four hours in his mind, visualizing the operation, seeing it all, down to the moment of triumph and success. He had done this countless times before, often in search of people he knew but mostly looking for strangers — which was worse, since he couldn't anticipate how they thought or what they might know about survival. The members of the lost party were Christians from a Bible camp in Portland, and because it was spring, Bill guessed, they had foolishly relied on a sense of the season's benevolence — climbing the mountain in lightweight gear, praising God as they went, and perhaps this snow, on Easter weekend, had reminded them of the Resurrection or the lamb or the wings of angels in flight. Bill Hughes had seen enough trailside cairns — he'd built a few himself from scree and talus and two crossed sticks — to know how futile it was to address a personal God in such situations.

For Bill, there was no such thing as being lost; there were only varying degrees of uncertainty. The party had left base camp two days ago — that meant seven thousand feet, maybe eight, eight-five. A margin of a thousand feet, two thousand at the most; the rule was, stay put. People driven on by hysterical hope weren't found until the summer thaw — bones, a jackknife or compass — or years later, frozen in their final attitude, hunched like fetuses in a womb of ice. Or they were never found — a dream, a thing to wonder about, forever. He'd made the ascent before, had stopped counting his climbs after one hundred, and he'd seen people — damned fools — do it in tennis shoes and shorts late in the summer. Hardly thinking, a scenario took shape: heavy spring snow would have a lot of creep, new wet snow contained little air, and he thought of breathing space, of chest compression, of snow rising up and then closing around the ribs like a vice.

Above Bill's nightstand, worked in crochet, hung a framed quote from Ben Franklin. "Some are weatherwise," it read. "Some are otherwise."

Dorothy had been through this before, too. Depending on the situation, and there were so many variables — variables of experience and age, faith and determination, sudden shifts in weather — Dorothy knew that hope lasted undiminished for twenty-four hours. She had learned this from Bill. Everyone had twenty-four hours — after that time, hypothermia was the big killer: falling body heat, slurred speech, memory lapses, uncontrollable shivering that slowly settled into a stunned numbness, loss of consciousness. "At a body temperature of ninety degrees," Bill had told her, "the heart only beats three times a minute." Twenty-four hours — beyond that time, hope and optimism were loans, borrowed notes that were often repaid in disappointment and regret long after. She knew about this, too. The letdown after a failed rescue was unbearable. All the women, the wives and members of the church guild, would gather in one house or another, preparing food for the men, aware of the helplessness, the poverty of their effort — brewing coffee, baking, fixing stew and sandwiches, answering phones, praying, waiting — the women did what they knew how to do, and none of it really mattered. They felt this, and the air was always charged with avoidance: the women spoke of garage sales, TV soaps, canning. Talking, they were like explorers searching for a low pass, some way around the mountain, which rose among them, looming in their midst like a kind of silence.

Dorothy wiped her hands on her apron and flicked on the radio. Their bedroom door shut. Bill pounded across the floor above. Dorothy listened as he lurched down the stairs, her heart synced to each descending step.

Bill stood in the doorway, filling the frame.

"Can I fix you something to eat?" Dorothy asked.

"I've got to go, Dot," Bill said. He was defending himself against her objections. He expected resistance; Dorothy didn't offer any. Bill kicked open the screen door and let it slap shut.

"There's no choice about it," he said.

"I understand," she said and reached in the sink and scrubbed another dish. She placed it to dry in the rack. Robins sang in the old, gnarled apple tree, a gray shadow in the backyard. Other things were becoming visible — the wheelbarrow on its side, the yellow webbing of a chaise, the blue rim of a plastic bucket. Silver pools had formed in the shallows after last night's heavy rain.

Bill turned his wife toward him and saw that she was crying. Her pain was a million miles away; he smudged a tear from her face with his thumb. Then he held his thumb to Dorothy's mouth, and Dorothy sucked the tear away, tasting the salt, feeling Bill's rough skin rasp her wet lip.

Bill lifted his hands and looked at them as though he were vividly picturing something he was holding. He dropped his empty hands. The scent of cold, wet cedar swept into the kitchen as he slammed the door shut. He gunned the truck in the driveway. Clouds of blue exhaust spewed from the tailpipe and the rumbling engine rocked the chassis like a cradle. While the engine warmed, Bill hurled logs from the woodpile into the bed, weighting it for traction. Lilac branches whipped his windshield as he sped away, turning onto the road toward town.

Dorothy leaned against the sink. She plunged her hands through the surface of graying suds and felt for another dish, but she was finished. She pulled the plug and watched the water suck down and vanish. Then she cleaned the drain trap.

Late in the afternoon, she caught a ride into town with Homer. All the storefronts had been decorated with Easter scenes, rabbits hopping through fields of green grass, a Jesus hovering above an empty tomb, ascending through the clouds. She felt the slight pressure of Homer's palm in the curve of her hip as he guided her across the street. The windows of the bar were blackened at sidewalk level except for a peephole in the shape of a diamond. Homer held the door for her. A few old men turned to the sudden light, squinting, then bending back down to their beers. Behind the bar, the grill spattered, thick smoke curling beneath the clogged vent. Dorothy had met the bartender once. Talbot? She didn't think so. A cousin, a nephew. He flipped a burger, then shuffled down along the bar, wiping a rag in the well. He said hello to Homer and looked at Dorothy.

"I'm Dorothy Hughes," she said. "Dot Hughes, Bill's wife — we met once."

"Dotty," he said, remembering. "Got some kids up there."

The other men looked up but turned away on contact. The bar had a drowsy, wartime feel; shame, lethargy, as only the unfit remained behind, isolated, knowing why.

"You heard anything?" Homer asked.

"Just the radio and the paper," the bartender said. "No calls, not so far."

He squeezed the rag dry, a trickle of rust-brown water. Dorothy ordered a hamburger. The bartender returned to the grill, flipped a burger, pressed grease from it. Over his shoulder, he said, "I'd expect something soon." He flattened two buns on sizzling pads of butter, speaking to himself now, into the weak updraft as the gray smoke fanned in lazy arabesques.

Homer went to the phone and made a call. Dorothy's plate came.

"On the house," the bartender said.

It felt good to eat. She ate slowly. The afternoon *Oregonian* was delivered and she examined a copy, the front page, the facts. She searched for familiar names among the list of the missing but found none. Her eyes scanned the bold black headline words, then sank between them, into the white spaces. She drew a picture of the mountain, gouged it out with a pencil. Inside it she wrote:

Dot

Dotty

Dorothy

She ordered another beer, and looked for Homer; he was still on the phone. This was where Bill would come, where the rescue team would come, after. If they failed, the men would stay on the mountain longer, two, three, sometimes four days, way beyond what was reasonable. They would be afraid to admit the truth, so they would remain up there, searching, grimly silent, determined, alone in their world. No one wanted to be the first to give in, and when they finally returned, past all delusions, they would keep together at a back table.

"I don't want you to go," Homer said.

"You?" Dorothy said. "It's impossible."

He nodded. "I'll send along what you need."

"I'll be fine."

She had only what was in her travel bag, in the locker. Her floats she'd left behind, and she knew Bill would take them down, begin dismantling her presence as he had Jacinta's, until there was no trace left of either of them. The kitchen, without the floats, would be a plain white room, a little shabby and small. Her very first float, a sea-worn shade of blue, she'd found nestled in a tangle of seaweed on the beach at Cape Alvarez; over the years, she'd picked up the floats in junk stores and flea markets and rummage sales, and she could still remember, for each, the day of discovery. Often she wondered what calamity had cut the float loose, what accident had torn the net, half a world away, so that the float would break free and drift in the current across the Pacific and finally wash ashore, a jewel found on the beach saved at someone's home, treasured for a while, and cast off again — she had always romanticized high seas and sharks and capsized trawlers.

The light outside the bar was shocking in its whiteness, and Dorothy stood for a moment, stunned and shielding her eyes. She crossed the street. In the waiting room, she found her travel bag. People were going places this weekend. It was Easter. A few little girls were dressed in frilly outfits, with white cotton tights and puffy skirts and dainty gloves, the fingertips of which were already smudged with diesel black dirt from everything they touched in the dingy station.

"I might come visit you," Homer said.

"Please." Dorothy lifted her travel bag.

"Bill's going to ask where you are. He'll want to know."

"Tell him whatever you think's right."

She boarded the bus and waved to Homer from her window. The bus pulled away from the curb, and she held a headrest to steady herself. As the bus rose out of the Gorge, toward the highway, and north, Dorothy watched the mountain. She knew little about what the men actually did up there. Often at lower elevations they used dogs, but in that high white country, swept by blizzard winds and blanketed in snow, trails of scent or sight were hard, if not impossible, to pick up, and when they were, they didn't last and were easily lost. She knew the men used long aluminum poles and ran them into the snow, plunged them down deep through the soft layers, hoping for contact, hoping to reach into something solid. Resistance gave them energy, kindled hope, often only to find a buried rock, cracked ice, earth. As time wore on, the slightest evidence gave life to the most outlandish expectations. Ruts and hollows appeared as footsteps wandering across the blank white fields and clouds shifting in the sky threw down swift dark shadows that seemed moving and alive. Drifts in the snow took on the shape of huddled bodies and the wind whistling over a rock outcropping was heard as a faint cry for help. Or, in those sudden, muffled silences that sometimes close over a mountain, when the wind dies and everything is held in a crystal quiet, a man might hear his own pulse and mistake it for the heartbeat of another.

ALL ABOARD

EARLIER THAT EVENING, I'd been experimenting, trying to make trees out of twigs and Norwegian lichen moss. Working in miniature sapped my patience, so when the kitchen door opened, and I heard Sarah crying, I took a time-out, a technique we've learned in our parenting class, closing my eyes and counting to ten before I opened them. She stood on the landing, quiet and still, the bright kitchen light casting her wide shadow down the basement stairs. I knew she wouldn't come down herself; very pregnant, Sarah hadn't seen the ground immediately below her in weeks, and the uneven risers and the wobbly slant of the steps were now too much to negotiate. I concentrated on setting up a spur and some siding for my model railroad, laying a Y-shaped section of track that veered off in two directions, one branch leading to a town I hoped to build someday, the other going nowhere, just a siding to park deadheads. My layout is N-scale, and I was hunched over, trying to slide those tiny miserable connectors together, when Sarah choked off a sob, and said: "It's for you, Neal."

"Who is it?" I asked.

"It's Mike," Sarah said.

I came upstairs.

"Yeah, Mike?"

"Neal, man — Flajole's dead."

I stood there, peeling back a corner of loose Formica on the countertop. The Formica curled and bent, stretching tendrils of old glue, then snapped off.

"No," I said. "You're joking."

"I wish I was," Mike said. "I wish."

I watched Sarah watch me. It was late. A bus gunned by outside. In twenty-three minutes, if the schedule held, there would be another. I was trying to remember how long it had been since I'd last seen Flajole — four years, five?

Mike was telling me what happened. Lately Flajole had been in the habit of buying himself a six-pack and driving until he was down to his last beer. Like a game, how far he'd go hinged on simple factors, variables of speed and thirst. Then he'd turn back and nurse that final beer all the way home, home being a run-down house he rented along the waterfront. According to Mike, the night Flajole died, he'd headed up into the mountains and was turning around at Snoqualmie Pass when he plowed his Volks through a barrier and down an embankment. His Bug tumbled down about a hundred feet, rolled over and over, righted itself, and caught fire. Flajole burned to death. He burned, they knew that, because he was still strapped to his seat, and the autopsy showed that everything vital was more or less intact.

"The funeral's tomorrow," Mike said.

I assumed the subject was closed and there was nothing more to say. I hung up. Sarah sipped her Sleepy-Time tea. She's sworn off caffeine.

"He called here last week," she said. "We talked."

The next day, as we dressed for the funeral, Sarah asked, "Why did it have to happen now of all times?"

"It has nothing to do with you, Sarah, so just get that idea out of your head." I tugged the narrow tongue of my tie until I felt the knot cinch against my throat. "Don't turn this into something it isn't," I said.

We arrived early. Some of the same nuns who taught us in grade school were already seated, rosary beads ticking away like knitting needles in the quiet church. I ushered Sarah to a pew near the front and then went outside to wait for the hearse. The white stones of St. Joseph's rose up through the gray morning fog and drizzle and bells rang out with the sleepy far-off sound of buoys. Flajole would have laughed to hear those bells ringing for him. I stood in the rain and watched the mourners file in, nodding to people I knew. The hearse pulled up against the curb, and the coffin slid forward on casters, an oyster-blue shell tricked out with silver detailing. Six of us carried it up the steps, waiting a moment in the rain as Father Thomas rattled the aspergillum, sprinkling the coffin with holy water. Then we escorted Flajole up the aisle, and I took my place beside Sarah.

It was a full-scale Catholic service: above us heavy beams joined like the arced ribbing of a ship's hull, and the full pews in the nave were arranged in rows like benches for galley slaves, and we were all sailing along with Flajole as cargo, and what there was to see in the offing we saw through colored windows, the same old stained glass scenery depicting Christ's Passion — Pilate's house in the back corner of the church, Mount Calvary in the front corner. Sister Celestine, our grade school principal, clutched both sides of the pulpit as she spoke, occasionally thumping her knuckle against the missal, and her eulogy carried above the fidgetings and cries and murmurs like the set narration of a tour guide, touching briefly upon the Catholic landmarks along the way.

I knew them all. St. Joe's was where we'd been baptized, where we first celebrated Mass, confessed our sins, received Communion, got confirmed, and, in a small ceremony five years ago, where Sarah and I were married. Now Flajole's funeral.

Only one thing was missing. The casket was closed, obviously, and there wouldn't be a viewing, but after I had lifted it, and felt how light it was, I kept thinking about what was left in there, about Flajole all burned up and black, stretched out on a bed of soft blue satin. I wondered if they'd crossed Flajole's hands in prayer and placed a crucifix between them. That would be proper, but Flajole wasn't a believer. I doubt he believed in anything but himself. I imagined he looked a lot like the mummy of a child prince I once saw in a museum, a shrunken thing, his flesh dark and twisted like a rope of beef jerky. Without a look at the body, though, the whole thing seemed unreal, a rehearsal; when the service ended, and Father Thomas shook smoke from the censer, waving sweet black clouds over the casket, it was like being diverted by some kind of crafty sleight of hand. I felt gypped and empty. I wanted the real thing. I wanted one last look at him.

Sarah joined me on the sidewalk. It was still raining, and in the gray air Sarah's face, framed in a black crepe scarf whose folds flowered around her like rose petals, seemed especially pale and drained.

"It wasn't so bad," she said. "I liked Sister Celestine's eulogy."

"Flajole would have hated it," I said. "He wouldn't have come."

"Well, he did," Sarah said.

The casket was in the hearse, rolled in so that it could be removed and carried feetfirst. At a proper Catholic observance, the deceased is dragged by his feet to the grave. I knew things like that. I had been an altar boy for eight years, serving at many Saturday funerals. Keeping the departed feetfirst distinguishes a funeral from the way we enter life at birth, where the smoothest delivery is headfirst. I knew this, too, because Sarah had just learned from the doctor that the baby we're expecting is upside down, a breech baby.

"What did *you* think?" Sarah asked.

"I don't know," I said. "It was fine, I guess."

"Don't act tough, Neal. I can't stand it right now." Sarah made a little adjustment to her scarf.

We walked to the parking lot. I turned on the headlights and followed the long train of cars going to the interment. At the cemetery, the casket was heaped with cut flowers, baskets, wreaths, bouquets — it looked like a parade float. I listened to the prayers, heard the sobs, supported Sarah when she broke down. Down the hill, I watched a backhoe dig another grave, the warm clumps of dirt expiring clouds of steam in the cool air.

On the way back to the reception, Sarah said, "It's creepy. When he called last week, we just talked. We had a conversation. A talk, you know? But now I'm thinking there was something more."

I watched the wiper blades cut through the rain. "What did you talk about?"

"Nothing."

"Was he dropping hints?"

"It's just something I felt," Sarah said. She drew a cross in the widening circle where her breath steamed the window. "Why did he call after so long? Just out of the blue?"

"What if Flajole hadn't died?" I asked. "What then? Would you still feel the same way?"

Sarah frowned, pressing her face to the window. "Does it have to keep raining like this?"

I leaned over and tried to kiss her.

"Please keep your eyes on the road."

At the reception I had a few cups of punch and talked with a lot of people I hadn't seen in years. I filled everyone in the best I could, using shorthand: wife, work, the baby we're expecting. I steered away from conversations about Flajole until Mrs. Flajole came up to me and clasped my hands.

"How are you, Mrs. Flajole?"

"I'm okay."

"I'm sorry."

"I know you are. You boys were good friends." Mrs. Flajole rummaged through her handbag. She was a big woman who had raised nine kids, mostly on her own. Mr. Flajole had been a derelict father; when he died, even his death had seemed an evasion, a cop-out. "I have something for you," Mrs. Flajole said, still fishing in her bag — the kind of enormous bag a mother of a large family gets used to, like an appendage. "I feel he's in a safe place, Neal. I felt it the night it happened. The minute the phone rang, I knew. A calm opened up inside me."

She handed me several photographs. "I thought you might want them for keepsakes." I thanked her, and then someone came over and swept Mrs. Flajole away into a private corner of the cafeteria. One photo showed us in a tree fort, another showed us acting like thugs on the hood of Flajole's car. I stuffed them in my coat pocket, and made a show of looking after Sarah, but she was nowhere in sight.

I found her in the church. She was kneeling at the Communion rail with her head bent and her hands folded. After a spell of wildness, Sarah became a strict believer. Her revived faith in the church strikes me as somewhat ironic, since it was I who suggested that we begin attending Mass again. She goes alone now. I started up the aisle toward Sarah, but decided to sit and wait in a back pew. An old reflex, I genuflected, and once I was down, I stayed there. I thought of my own faith, which has gone the way of the tooth fairy — in the beginning it was fun and profitable, something to look forward to, and then it compensated for things I lost, and now, as I look back, I see that it was all just child's play, a shell game of sorts, so that these days when I put my head on my pillow, facing up to the darkness above, I hope for nothing more than a good night's rest.

After Flajole was buried, Sarah began attending daily Mass. The first few mornings she was up and out of the house before I woke and while she was away I'd start coffee and make breakfast and dillydally over the newspaper. This went on for several days until one morning I got up extra early and waited for Sarah in the kitchen. When I asked her why she was going to Mass, she stated flatly that for every cause there was an effect.

"I'm trying to build up good causes," she said.

I sipped my coffee and looked out the window. Eight months ago, when I learned that Sarah was pregnant, I didn't exactly suggest abortion. I didn't say it. What I did was question aloud whether or not we could really afford to have a kid. Were we ready, was this the time? In my mind, the blind, immediate answer was no, but I have not been forgiven for my moment of doubt over this, our first child, and Sarah, now well into her final trimester, carries the baby like a badge and a rebuke — a badge of her faith, a rebuke to mine. Because of this, I've put off choosing a possible name, refusing to discuss it, but Sarah says if the baby's a boy she's going to name him after me. Neal Junior.

"You don't have to stare out the window, Neal. Don't waste your time pretending you're thinking things over because I know you don't agree."

Sarah poured herself a cup of coffee, brought it to

her lips, and then dumped it down the drain. "Old habit," she said. "I miss a cup of coffee in the morning."

"One cup won't kill you," I said.

Sarah was right, this cause-and-effect thing seemed superstitious to me. Rapidly we reached the point where we could no longer watch the nightly news: a plane crash in Madrid or a violent coup in some crazy country no one's ever heard of would shoot pangs of negativity from the tube to her womb. There were signs, there were omens. One particularly harassed morning I learned that even burnt toast adversely affected the destiny of our unborn child. A piece of sourdough bread wedged in the coils of the toaster, and by the time I jabbed it free with the knife, black smoke swarmed so thickly through our tiny kitchen we couldn't breathe. I opened the back door for circulation, and when the air cleared, Sarah announced, as if she'd seen a sign, that we had to begin the exercises right away.

"Dr. Harrelson says there's a good chance we can get the baby to turn around if we do them every day," she said.

That the baby was a breech baby, headed in the wrong direction, so to speak, only fueled her imagination. A breech baby is not serious, in a life-threatening sense; advanced medical science can take care of the problem. Still, after that morning, we began a series of exercises that would help get the baby's head properly oriented. There was also a vial of herbal essence Sarah picked up from some acupuncturist in Chinatown — a placebo I applied to her toes. Then Sarah, going off to Mass and celebrating Communion, attended to the state of her soul and, I'm guessing, my soul, wiping the slate clean and absolving the unborn infant of the burdens of the world: by the due date, our child would have a stockpile of good causes and a fresh start, a running, headlong leap at life, except for the usual blemish, original sin, which baptism would mop away, posthaste. Just in case, besides the exercises and the routine of daily Mass, Sarah began doing other things too. She started writing good words on scraps of paper. "Unity" and "Abundance" and "LIFE!" were pinned to the fridge with pineapple magnets.

As the rift between us widened, my first impulse was to try redirecting her thoughts. Then, by way of atonement and to show remorse, I decided to keep my distance, and never complain or argue. Outwardly, I retreated into what we have now, stalemate. Actually, I began to enjoy the freedom and solitude I found in the hours she was out of the house. Mass began at six A.M. Work — right now I make decent money painting houses — never started before nine, and so every morning I'd perform the exercises, see Sarah off, make coffee, grab my cigarettes, go downstairs, and tinker with my model railroad until eight o'clock, roughly, when it was time to load the car with the tools I'd need for the day.

Although we rent the house we live in, a while back, after a year of hesitation and delay, I made the decision to go ahead and build a more or less permanent train layout in the basement, figuring I could deal with dismantling it when the time came. It's a fair-sized basement, big enough to accommodate the four four-by-eight sheets of particleboard my tracks sprawl over. So far, I've painted the boards forest green and laid down nearly one hundred feet of track on a ballast of aquarium gravel. I've built a range of snowcapped mountains out of papier-mâché and painted a blue river that winds diagonally across the layout and eventually empties into the darker blue of the sea. There's one lonely little depot, around which, at some point, I hope to build my town, at the base of the mountains. I still need many things — trees, cars, roads, trestles, tunnels, signals, farms, houses, people, stores, factories — but a lot of this stuff, though small, is expensive, especially if you hope to do a first-class job, with any sort of attention to realistic detail. I know I can't do it all at once, but I don't mind. I get great pleasure simply thinking about it, and planning how it will be, when at last it's all done.

All my life I've loved trains. As a kid I read historical romances about crossing the continent, about Leland Stanford driving the golden spike at Promontory, Utah, about the fabulous fortunes amassed by men like James J. Hill. Sometimes I take Sarah and a picnic lunch to a park north of Seattle carrying a pocketful of pennies and nails to flatten on the tracks when the afternoon Empire Builder passes. Other times, I'll sit alone on the overpass in Ballard and watch the Burlington Northern freights rumble out of the yard, four or five engines lugging the huge length of train, the slack couplings jerking tight, slapping down the line like dominoes, the whistle wailing sadly as the locomotives take on speed. I always wave like a maniac to the engineer and the brakeman as they roll under me. Part of it's sheer excitement, part of it's study: watching trains, I find things I can apply to my layout. I love freight trains and passenger trains equally, and if I were given the chance, I bet I'd enjoy even a short ride on a subway; among the many fond memories I have of our honeymoon, I have to admit that the most exciting moment was the elated surge of anticipation I felt as Sarah and I rode the Amtrak out of the King Street Station, up to Vancouver for a weekend at the World's Fair.

Earlier tonight as we washed dishes Sarah began to shudder and then her whole body convulsed and she dropped a coffee cup on the floor, shattering it. We'd eaten dinner mostly in silence. It was my night to dry. I stood behind Sarah, ready with the towel. I saw the first quiet shudder start up through her shoulders, a slight ripple that rolled into a wave. It could've been anything — her sudden reflection in the dirty suds, the way I held the towel. Had the coffee cup not crashed, I would have let it ride.

"Don't move, Sarah," I said.

"Oh my God," she cried. "My God!"

She put her hands over her face and screamed.

"It's just a cup. Don't get excited."

As I reached for the broom, Sarah fell to her knees and clasped her belly.

"Sarah?"

She wouldn't answer. A maroon drop of blood smeared on the linoleum where she knelt. Sarah was crying and throwing her head back and forth, strands of hair tangled up in her mouth. She was unreachable. I bent down and held her face, forced her to look me in the eye. "What's happened?" I said. "What's wrong?" She bit down on her hand. "Damnit, Sarah, is the baby okay?"

"Yes, the baby's okay. It's not the baby, all right?"

"Then what is it, Sarah?"

"Oh man," she said.

Her foot was bleeding. I told her.

She said, "It's not supposed to be this way, Neal."

I helped Sarah hop over to the kitchen table. She sat down, and I tweezed a porcelain sliver from her foot. I gently dabbed the wound with a wet towel, and pressed a Band-Aid over it. When I finished, she started crying again.

"What is it, Sarah? What's going on?"

"I can't tell you, Neal. How can I tell you?"

"Just tell me."

"I can't."

"Come on, Sarah —"

Sarah rose and limped to the living room. I got a glass of water. When I came in, she was sitting on the sofa, twirling a cushion's frayed thread around her finger, pulling it so tight her flesh turned pale. I offered her the water.

"Neal," she said. "Do you think about Flajole?"

"Yeah. Sometimes."

"It doesn't seem like you do."

"I had a dream about him one night."

"What was the dream?"

"Take a sip of water, okay?"

Sarah drank some of the water. I could hear her gulp. Around me on the floor there lay a scattering of kid's toys we'd already purchased, stuffed animals, balls, blocks, plastic cars and trucks. Records leaned against the stereo the way Sarah liked them, outside their dust jackets. Now wasn't the time to say anything.

"So?"

"It wasn't much of a dream. Pretty goofy, really."

"Just say it."

"Okay, here goes." I closed my eyes for a minute, getting a picture. "Flajole was working on a car outside our house. A wild-ass VW, with this elaborate exhaust system. One wheel was off, and there was another small one in front, and two big wheels in back. Out of nowhere, he told me, 'I tried to quit smoking once. Seventh grade. It was hard. Don't laugh,' he said. He said that in the dream — 'Don't laugh.' But I don't remember laughing."

I tapped out a cigarette, and then slipped it back in the pack. At least until the baby's born, I'm only supposed to smoke in the basement, or outside on the back porch.

"You can smoke," Sarah said. "Go ahead, smoke."

I continued. "Anyway, then he said, 'I used to stay up all night and there was nothing to do. I couldn't sleep. There were these animals that fly at night.' That's all he said, but I knew right away the animals were bats. We started throwing pennies up in the air. The bats dove for them, thinking they were insects. I asked Flajole, 'You don't know anyone who's got a VW for sale?' I told him I didn't want anything fancy or souped up, nothing like the one he was working on. Just stock. He smiled. The next thing, I could see bats coming down from the mountains."

"And?"

"That was it."

I lit a cigarette.

Sarah asked, "What does it mean?"

I don't usually waste time dwelling on my dreams, but about this one I had a few rough ideas. "To me," I said, "there's a few obvious things. One is that Flajole, in the dream, is working on a Volkswagen, and that's the car he died in."

"Flajole was always working on Bugs. He was known for that."

"True. But this VW needed work, and then he tells me he tried to quit smoking. I take that as an admission of something. I don't know what — maybe that he wanted to change. To fix himself like he was fixing the car."

Sarah switched a lamp on low. Outside it was dark, the deep, sudden dark that comes early in fall. It was quiet, too. We live in a neighborhood where people quiet down and go to sleep at a regular hour.

"He was afraid," Sarah said. "He was afraid of the bats."

"Flajole wasn't afraid, Sarah. I never saw him afraid of anything."

"Nope, sorry, Neal. You're wrong. He always made too big a show of it. He was a show-off. When people have to insist that much, it's because they're hiding something."

This wasn't true. At times Flajole lived in his car, and for a while he lived in a garage, Ransom's garage, on Aloha Street. He parked his car on one side and slept on the other side in a bed, just a mattress on skids, really. You don't let yourself live that way if you're scared.

"Well," I said, "I think the bats came into the dream

because bats have radar. They can see at night. Flajole died at night, probably because he couldn't see. Remember, in the end I see all those bats up in the mountains — up where Flajole died."

"But the bats go after the pennies," Sarah said. "They don't know what they're doing. They make mistakes."

"Flajole made a mistake too."

"You know what I think? I think Flajole was death."

I stubbed my cigarette and reached for another.

"Maybe he didn't want to be, maybe he realized it wouldn't go anywhere. But he was death in your dream."

"I don't know, Sarah. That seems like a stretch to me."

"It's not, Neal. He tells you he tried to quit smoking and you laugh at him. In the dream, you know he's death. And you're not. That's why you laugh at him. That's why you don't want a car like his. You're not him. You don't really want death." She looked at me. "Remember, Neal, it's your dream. You're the one dreaming."

At this, Sarah folded her hands over her face and cried softly to herself. Then she cried harder. She sat heavily on the sofa, her legs spread out wide, her feet square on the floor, just flopped there in the way pregnant women have. My dream about Flajole dissolved before me, reborn as an elaborate lesson about the sanctity of life.

"He was my first."

"What?"

"Before you, Neal."

I knew this. It wasn't news.

"That's what I think about when I think about him. That's what I pray about at church."

"You slept with Flajole, right?"

Sarah nodded.

"But I know all this, Sarah. It was a long time ago."

"It wasn't love," she said. "It wasn't you."

"How many times?" I asked. "How many times wasn't it love?"

"Don't be stupid, Neal." She wiped her eyes, deep blue glassy marbles. "Listen to me."

I nodded. "I'm listening."

"Neal?"

"Yes, Sarah?"

Sarah held herself, held her belly. Sarah looked up.

"I already know," I said. "I've always known."

"What do you mean?"

"You know what I mean. He got you pregnant." I had cruelly hoped she would use the word, say it, but looking at her I lost heart. "You had an abortion."

Sarah said nothing. I don't know what it was, the cruelty. I guess I wanted to leave behind Sarah's world of good words and cosmic hocus-pocus. I didn't have to say it again, but I did, with relish. I wanted that word out.

"You had an abortion."

We faced each other in a silence that hardened. We could have been two stones. I didn't think we'd ever move. In general you hope the truth will come out, that eventually, in your life, it will show up. Then it does. So what? Where do you go after you know the truth?

"I didn't use to believe," Sarah said. She got up and went to sleep.

*   *   *

It was well past midnight. The stars in the sky were sharp and clear, the air crisp enough for a light frost to dust the lawns and whiten the windshields of the cars along our street. I stopped at a mini-mart for cigarettes. In the parking lot someone had hit a duck, a male mallard with an iridescent green head and neck that lit up in my low beams as I pulled in to park. With winter coming, that duck should've flown south by this time.

Inside I bought two packs of Marlboros.

"You got a dead duck out there," I said to the man.

The man, who looked sleepy, said, "What should I do?"

I shook my head. "I don't know."

"Anything else?" the man asked.

"Hold on." I went to the cooler and grabbed a six of Rainiers. "That's it," I said.

I drove across the lake and wound around a maze of cloverleafs and finally hit the main highway. As soon as I left the suburbs behind, plunging into country darkness, I lit a cigarette and cracked a beer. The land was low and rolling, dairy farms mostly, with barns and silos silhouetted on knolls like ships cresting a wave. For cheap fun Sarah and I used to pack a big lunch and get in the car and take day-trips through this area. The back roads were in good shape, smooth and twisting, great to cruise over, and the landscape was scenic, so that it didn't matter where we went or if we lost our way for a while. On one of these trips we accidentally discovered a small farm between Fall City and Carnation, a U-pick place where we ended up getting three huge flats of blueberries.

I had already driven by it when Sarah said to stop and go back.

"What for?" I said.

"Did you see that place? Turn around. You have to see this."

We drove underneath a gateway and parked in the gravel lot. The farm was operated by a retired Boeing machinist, a funky old man in bib overalls and a gray beard trimmed like a troll's, with no hair on his upper lip. His wife wore overalls too, and tied her shaggy yellow hair beneath a red sun-faded scarf. The old man had a few wooden donkeys, some ceramic deer, a working windmill, a pond stocked with bass, and a sheltered arbor of white lattices hung with grapevines. Inside the arbor, there were wrought iron benches with wood slats to sit at. A bridge arched over the pond and in the middle of it a clay black guy sat fishing. On the lawn, two plastic squirrels were eating acorns.

No one else was there, and we decided to stay. Sarah and I lost track of time. We worked up and down the rows, moving along the stamped dirt paths, eating some of the blueberries and storing the rest in cardboard containers. We picked until it began to rain. We were about to quit, when the old man found us in one of the back rows. "Just wait it out," he said.

We sat under the shelter and ate our sack lunch, speculating about the old man and woman's sex life. Sarah imagined it to be completely fantastic, to involve costumes, strange props. The pond came alive under the falling rain, a few circles spreading out slowly across the surface, overlapping, and then the whole thing boiling when the rain really fell hard. We tasted some more of our blueberries, bursting ripe with tiny slits in the skin. I remember the juice stains on Sarah's fingers. Dark purple lines ran in the wrinkles and the cuticles dyed indigo, showing against the white bread as she held her sandwich.

"We'll never use all these," Sarah said. She looked at the three flats and started laughing. "What are we going to do with all these damn blueberries?" She sprayed a handful into the pond. "Make a wish," she said. "A blue wish."

I closed my eyes and waited a few seconds. I listened to the rain. Then I pitched the berries.

"What was your wish?"

"I can't tell. You don't tell or else it won't come true."

"That's not true," Sarah said. "Tell me your wish, Neal."

I hesitated, then tried to make something up, but I was so happy, I drew a blank.

Past the Fall City turnoff, farmland gave way to foothills, soft hills that were densely forested and dark enough to make the high cloud cover, gathering as I headed east, seem pale and luminous in comparison, as though soaked in moonlight. Soon I was winding up through deep clefts in the hills and couldn't see much for all the trees crowding against the road. The radio surged in and out of range, and a sea of static washed over the frequency. I turned the knob and when I got a clear signal I settled back in my seat, half listening, half thinking of Flajole.

The last time I saw Flajole was the night we stole an engine to replace the one he'd blown in his ratty gray Bug, the car everybody called the Mole. He'd cruised Queen Anne Hill every night for a week in his brother's truck, scoping out the situation, checking the odometer reading with the serial number on the engines of every Volks on the hill. He said he wanted to make sure he was getting an original and not some half-breed rebuilt motor. Flajole was very deliberate that way, and his search paid off. He found just the thing he was looking for, a forty-horse engine, 1967. The last good engine Volkswagen made, according to Flajole. They got too complicated afterwards, he said, and that was bad in his book, the worst thing. Adding vacuum advances, automatic chokes, and various filters made the late-model engines respond sluggishly and also robbed the Volks of its genius, which was simplicity.

We were at a party and I was blasted, talking to Sarah, in fact, who wasn't my wife yet, who wasn't even my girlfriend yet, although I had designs. Like I said, in those days Sarah had a reputation for being kind of wild, and while her bold reputation attracted me as an offering of freedom, I also cast myself in the role of reformer. I think I thought that together we might have the best of both worlds. Anyway, I remember *Dark Side of the Moon* was on the stereo — Pink Floyd was always on the stereo then — and Flajole was suddenly at my side, yanking on my coat sleeve. He said hello to Sarah and smiled. He was nothing to look at — average height, a little peanut head, puffy eyes always red from dope, hands permanently blackened with grime. Even then he was a grease monkey.

Flajole smiled at Sarah again, winking, and said, "He'll be back."

"You gotta help me," he said as he started the truck. He slipped a joint from inside a hollow pressure gauge, handed it to me, and punched the lighter. The joint was rolled in yellow wheat straw, his trademark. A faded tree freshener swayed from the rearview mirror and gave the truck the thick stink of a gas station bathroom.

"Where are we going and what am I doing?" I asked. I looked behind us as we climbed the steep grade up Queen Anne Hill and saw the lights of the city losing resolution and blurring into clusters of blue and yellow.

"The less you know," he said, "the better."

Flajole hit the joint, squinting. "Now, down this street I'm gonna park the truck and walk a little ways. You just sit tight. Don't do anything, don't even think. Just sit."

"Man, Flajole," I said. I hit the joint and passed it.

"Nothing's gonna happen to you," he said. "Nothing's gonna happen to anyone."

Flajole eased the truck against the curb.

"I'm just gonna do this thing," he said. "You hang loose here until I give a signal, then pull the truck forward, all right?" He got out and then leaned in through the window. "Get in the driver's seat, buddy." Flajole grabbed a scissor jack from the truck bed and stuffed his pockets with tools. He walked down the sidewalk doing his imitation of a citizen out for an evening stroll, and then disappeared in the space between street lamps, reappeared briefly, and vanished.

I sat in the truck and toked the roach, straining my eyes into the darkness where I imagined Flajole would be when he finished and gave the signal. I was stoned, and time stopped as I sort of blanked out. The truck was parked in front of a small square house, windows faintly lit a shade of dull gold behind thick coarse curtains. I thought I saw a shadow drift behind one of the windows. I was afraid of who might be behind there and to calm down I told myself, you are just doing this thing. A porch light flipped on and a man stepped out. He lit a cigarette, glowing as he cupped the flaring match to his face. Then he took up a tumbler of whiskey, swirling it in circles before he sipped. Moths tapped against the bulb above him, the light flickered with shadows, and the man seemed to be surveying his life, taking stock, savoring it. Nothing is going to happen to you, I kept repeating. Just sit tight and don't even think. The man's ice clinked against his glass. A car passed. Then the man spun his cigarette into the shrubs, knocked back his drink, and went inside, leaving the porch light on.

If I'm remembering my life right, after that night Flajole and I drifted apart. A year later I got married. I went to college for two years and took accounting classes because they were practical. I worked on a minor in history because I liked it. At some point I felt the haul through school was too long, and started painting houses full-time. Flajole worked for a car dealership downtown, overhauling Volkswagens, and now and then he'd call me, but I never went out with him again. So the last time I saw him was five, going on six years ago — going on forever, the way it turned out.

But that night, Flajole was flagging me in the middle of the street. I eased the brake down and rolled ahead with the lights off. He waved me forward until I pulled parallel with a red Volkswagen. He held his palms out flat. "You dreaming?" he said. "Let's go, chop chop. Leave the motor running."

We hoisted the body of the car up over the engine, gripping the bumper on either side. With the engine ripped out, the gutted shell was surprisingly light. Flajole had dropped the engine down through the floor of the car, resting it on the scissor jack; we got it into the bed of the truck, sliding it up a ramp of two-by-fours propped against the tailgate.

As we drove away, I kept an eye out behind us.

"Only four bolts hold a VeeWee engine in place," Flajole said as we turned down the hill. "Snip a few wires, and it's yours."

My ears popped from the changing pressure, and then at the pass the road leveled out. I made a U-turn onto the opposite shoulder and set my emergency flashers.

I slid a beer into my coat pocket and grabbed a flashlight from the glove compartment. The night was cold, a good deal below freezing, with a trace of blue snow swirling across the road. I walked along the guardrail, searching for the place where Flajole plunged through. The flashlight flickered on and off, depending on the angle I held it at. Behind me, a truck ground into a downshift. Tiny yellow reflectors on the rail winked like cat eyes. About a hundred yards from where I parked, the railing tore away and there was a ragged hole where the metal bent back sharply and snapped. Over the edge, the shoulder dropped off suddenly, falling down a rocky hill until it flattened somewhat and hit a brake of trees. I put the flashlight in my pocket and climbed down the embankment, sort of tumbling on my butt the last ten feet or so.

The wind blowing through the trees kept the world a whisper away from silence. Flajole's car leaned up against the trees, this scorched pod, entirely blackened except where loose snow shook from the branches and sifted down, the frozen crystals sparkling like sugar on the rooftop and hood. I circled it. All the windows were shattered, but the tires were still good. I gave them a kick. I went clear around the car and then I sat on the rear bumper, looking back up the hill to the road, and across the road to the mountain, high up where the dark tree line ended abruptly, clean-shaven, and the crown was capped in white. It seemed unlikely to me that Flajole would goof up a U-turn and drive over the embankment by accident. Too many things would have to come together in a single moment for that to happen: velocity, angle, location, and then the mistake that somehow fit and glued all those pieces into the cup of Flajole's fate. Hit and run was a better possibility, or simply an oncoming car taking the turn too wide and forcing Flajole off the road at a point along the way that just happened to be fatal. But a plain accident was out of the question.

The cloud cover broke apart as it rose and sailed eastward over the peaks, and a milky wash of moonlight showered down in the gaps. With the sky clearing the air

cooled and cut sharply through my jacket. I moved around
to the front of the car. The beaked hood was partially eaten
away by explosion. The gas tank in a Volkswagen is in
front and the fire must have ignited there under the hood
and shot up through the firewall. Is it true that the end
gives life shape, defines it? That's what I thought when I
studied history. I tried to imagine Flajole starting down
the pass, slamming the gears forward, gathering speed, but
I couldn't picture it. I didn't think his death was an accident, but I wouldn't say he died on purpose either.
What's in between? Sarah would answer: God's mysterious
will, the divine plan, some voodoo providence.

I lit a cigarette and drank some of my beer. I looked
through the windshield. The interior was black and melted
to hell. The upholstery was all gone and the seats were
just a nest of springs and the gearshift knob hung to the
side of the stem like a toasted marshmallow. Plastic boils
lifted off the go-cart steering wheel, and the custom gauges
Flajole installed to measure rpm's and oil temp had popped
their glass and left nothing but holes in the dash. On the
driver's side, the door hung off its hinge, jacked open with
a pry bar. I stepped in. The air inside had a burnt metallic
taste. I depressed the clutch, floored the gas, stomped the
brakes, jerked the steering wheel. Flajole, I thought, you
bat-blind dead bastard. I found a screwdriver and pried
open the glove compartment. Everything in there was preserved: a road map of the U.S., a few tapes, and a tire
gauge. I unscrewed the tire gauge — hollow, a joint
slipped out, rolled in yellow wheat straw, as always.

I lit the joint off my cigarette.

"Fla-jole!"

My voice echoed back at me, a silly, shrinking sound. I shut my eyes and smoked. Around the last time I saw Flajole, he'd lost his apartment and was staying in Potter's garage, looking for something else. He hadn't lived at home for three years. I'm not sure why, but he refused to go back. "They're history" was all he'd say. We were nineteen. After we stole the engine, Flajole and I took some beers out to a lover's leap, an overlook. He backed the truck up to the edge of the cliff where a tall leafy oak jutted out over the empty air, it's dry turning leaves rustling in the wind. We sat on the tailgate, dangling our legs, and below us the city spread away, hill after hill sparkling with lights like receding waves on a late August night, jumping with phosphorescence. Flajole showed me all the things he planned to do to the engine, how he would increase its efficiency and horsepower just by simplifying it, getting it reduced to its essence.

"Get rid of the vacuum advance," Flajole said, pointing to the distributor. "Mechanical's rougher, but better."

"G-monk," I said. "I can't believe you did it."

"I can tear down one of those suckers in an hour."

"That's not what I mean."

"Glad you came along?" Flajole laughed. "I didn't think you would. That's why I didn't say anything."

Never in my life had I considered what Flajole saw in me. As a kid I was fascinated by the lives of powerful men, men who nudged history just enough to lend their names to it — the railroad magnate James J. Hill, the story goes, rode across Montana along the Great Northern route drawing names from a hat, randomly assigning those exotic names to depot towns: Malta, Glasgow, Havre, names of favorite places he'd encountered in his world travels. But in the wide galaxy of people, I'm not that spectacular, not a man to set off shock waves through the universe. There's an orbital steadiness to the things I do, and perhaps what I have, at best, is the capacity to be decent, to behave in a way that other men can predict. A man parks his car at night, he expects the engine to be there in the morning. That's life to me. Yet the night we stole that engine I just washed my hands of it. Flajole was powerful, in a way, and I liked being with him, but I had no sense of why he liked me.

We sat above the city. We sat and drank, and we talked.

"You're into Sarah, huh?"

"I think so."

I'd only been out with Sarah once, officially. It still filled me with excitement to hear her name spoken aloud. When I heard it, I saw her blue eyes and the smoothness of her skin up close.

"You don't mind?" I asked.

Flajole said, "Hell no."

"What happened?"

"She told me not to tell anyone," he said.

"You got her pregnant."

"I can't comment."

"Am I right?"

"Maybe you'll get married. Maybe you'll live down there," Flajole said. He hoisted his beer in a sweeping gesture out toward the city, taking it all in. "Huh? One of those little lights yours?"

We were pretty drunk by this time, and I was feeling giddy, like nothing much mattered. The sky was beginning to shift from black to a washed-out gray smear.

"Huh?" he said, standing up. "Go ahead, pick one, Neal, point it out. We got the truck, my tools, I'm in the mood."

Flajole jumped off the tailgate to a low branch of the oak. He inched his way to the end of the branch and swung there laughing out over space and I laughed too. Then he hung himself upside down by his knees and beat his chest. The limb bent, the leaves quivered. His T-shirt slipped down over his face and some nickels and pennies and foil gum wrappers fell from his pockets.

"Toss me a beer, Neal."

The first beer sailed past him, tumbling down the hill. Flajole caught the second beer, cracked it open, and drank, hanging there. I climbed onto the limb and cradled myself against the trunk.

"What should we do tomorrow?" Flajole asked.

I opened a beer and drank it down. The wind blew and Flajole rocked back and forth on the branch, beer spilling off his face, his hair, splashing away. I remember thinking: I'm up in a tree, an accessory to a crime, and a wild woman loves me. An outlaw, a desperado, I'd stepped outside my life. The whole city spread out below us and I could see a ferry crossing Puget Sound, its yellow lighted windows glowing against the glassy pale gray water, moving slowly away from us, towards the dark headlands of Bainbridge Island. "It is tomorrow," I said.

Flajole crushed his beer can and let it fall. He swung himself upright, rocking the limb with his legs. He tapped out two cigarettes, lit them, and passed one to me. Flajole drew hard and exhaled.

"What should we do now?" he asked.

I opened my eyes. A gust of wind kicked up, whistling through the cracked windshield, and the smell of scorched metal and charred material was sharp in the cold air. Peeled paint and ash flaked like black snow from the rooftop. I toked the roach until a seed exploded and it fell apart in my lap. Funny, in a reflex of habit I brushed the embers away quickly, afraid I'd burn something. I was stoned. I was getting cold. I had to start moving. I ran my flashlight around the car once more. A plastic Jesus dripped down off the dash like a lump of black Velveeta. I remembered him, one of those standard, tacky Jesuses. Flajole always pinched his arms with a collection of feathered roach clips. I tapped the rearview mirror with my flashlight. Most of the mirror was gone, but a few cracked pieces still hung in there, blackened by smoke and streaks of melted plastic. I decided to keep the pressure gauge, a souvenir. I sat there, frozen, and then I thought I heard a branch snap.

Back on the road, I turned around and made my final farewell. I was surrounded by mountains, a deeper darkness heaving against the dark sky. I drank the last of my beer. I balanced myself on the guardrail, took a few teetering steps, and stopped. The wind blew sharply, but I hung there a moment. Far down the hill, a slice of bumper chrome shone, grinning. I wanted to sum things up, add my own little euology, but I wasn't getting anywhere: I felt like I had with Sarah at the blueberry farm, drawing a blank. I threw my empty can over the embankment. I listened to it tumble down over the rocks until it came to rest and everything was silent again.

I look over my layout, the wide green expanse of it. From a window well a beam of light, solid with drifting, falling motes of dust, slants down over my papier-mâché mountain, like a little sunrise, a tiny day beginning at my train depot. It's a traditional depot, vintage chalet-style, the kind where the conductor steps out onto a platform, cups his hand, and shouts, "All aboard!" I crank the transformer up and my train chugs toward it. I notch up the speed. Someday I'll start to build my town, and in that town there will be a few small houses and some small people, dogs and cats, streets and cars, and stoplights with crossing guards, and a row of storefronts, including a dime store and a lunch counter, with an old guy who does nothing but regale everyone with hilarious stories, and there will be a church, a church on a hill, overlooking everything, and of course, my river, blue as blue can be, divides the town.

Upstairs I hear the sounds of the day beginning, of water flowing as Sarah showers, and I know that soon, given last night, she'll be off to church, praying with renewed fervor for holy intercession on behalf of our baby. I light a cigarette. Sarah comes down from the bedroom, stomping heavily. She walks like a cowpoke these days. I hear her cross the kitchen floor. The basement door inches open.

"Neal?"

I listen.

"Neal?"

I'm deciding what I think.

"Neal, if you're down there, and you're okay, just say so."

I can do that. "I'm okay."

She stays there, and I know why. I come upstairs. We move wordlessly into the darkened living room and Sarah lies on her back. A bus goes by. I scrunch her sweatshirt up over her breasts, moons of pale white arched and spilling above the lace fringe of her bra. Sarah shuts her eyes and breathes softly, her stomach swelling, girded with winding blue veins. In a clockwise rotation, I begin to knead her belly, white and warm as rising dough, one revolution after another, hand over hand, helping the baby turn, turn and navigate its way, borne safely by the current, down, I guess. The doctor could perform a C-section but the menace and violence inherent in the scalpel are something Sarah prefers to avoid if possible. She is right, violence is no way to begin a life. I try to imagine the motions I make on the surface setting off a current of small waves within, a tidal rhythm of swirls unrolling in a world that's never silent.

Sarah says, "You believe everything's going to be okay, don't you?"

I keep my hands working. What is happening? Little by little, imperceptible if examined too closely, but fluent and moving and destined, the child turns.

I ask, "Four weeks?"

"Maybe three."

There is time. From where I kneel Sarah's stomach appears taut and smooth as a drumhead. I glide my fingers over the rounded surface, a marvel of accommodation. I'm thinking Sarah's imagination is an act of faith when the baby kicks. A faint thump, it's almost not there, but then another follows, there, there, there, in the palm of my hand, so insistent I'm tempted to pull away. I imagine these swimming kicks make a concussion within; I press my ear to the place and though the sound seems far away and muted the softness of the report in no way cushions the reprimand I feel. I listen, echoes, repercussions, then leave a wet christening kiss behind when I sit up. "Neal," Sarah says, touching the warm, moist spot.

"I want this baby bad," she says.

"Me too," I say.

Outside, I hear another bus go by, on schedule. Our eyes open and we see each other wavering through water. Sarah wipes her eyes and rises, correcting herself. "See you later, Neal." The door clicks shut and she's gone.

I fix a pot of coffee. While it brews, I wander through the house, putting away the toys, pairing my records with their long-lost sleeves, emptying ashtrays, and collecting stray glasses. In another month or so we'll be a family of three — it dawns on me that that time is already here, that we are three now. We will need a bigger house. I stand in the living room. My eyes hurt and everything around me looks kind of stripped down and shabby in the first morning light. Our house is small, what in Seattle is called a spite house, half a house built on half a lot. A house built in spite of the limitations. I've never been anywhere long enough to know, but they may be called that elsewhere. Sarah negotiates the front steps, moving toward the car. Watching her, I run my fingers over the window moldings, feeling how they flake in places to reveal other coats and colors. She opens the car door. Then I close the curtains. She won't be home for an hour, and I figure this morning the solace of shutting the curtains is a little thing I can give myself, in the meantime. Then I hear the engine start.

LYRICISM

OCTOBER

POTTER WAS OUT in the middle of the stream, standing on a huge rock. He'd been standing there all morning, and a good part of the afternoon, casting without results. There was a riffle of white water below him, and a glassy pool on the far bank, recessed and overhung with a lattice of branches, of flickering light and shadows, where he could see his dappled reflection in the fading light. As the day and the river darkened, so had Potter's reflection, and what he saw — as he lifted his hand, now, right now — was a man on a rock, waving to himself.

Hello.

Good-bye.

Jane had gone a while ago. She had walked back to their cottage, about a mile away, and left him to fish, while she packed and settled up with the florid, bustling German woman who owned the place. Potter and Jane had been up in the Adirondacks on reprieve from city life for three days. After seeing the colors, the fall foliage, there hadn't been much to do; it was October, and Lake Placid was mostly shut down, and when it was open, it was tasteless and overpriced. Jane bought Potter a cheap rig at a roadside tackle shop, a flimsy, plastic rod and reel, some flies and sinkers, because the river was there, and because this trip was her idea, and Potter imagined that she felt responsible, and hated to see him unhappy.

The shadowy hills sloped gently toward him, but he was severely hungover, and the incline of forest seemed steeper than it was, and the rapids assaulted his ears, sounding cavernous and terribly swift. He couldn't face the rushing white water for long without a touch of dizziness. It was nice, though, concentrating on the fishing. He cast upstream, and watched the line sweep toward him, and then past him, downriver. He reeled in, the thin clear line cutting a faint V against the water. He cast again, and sat down to smoke a cigarette.

The dark pool across the river struck Potter as a likely place for fish. He didn't know why, exactly. He wasn't much of a fisherman. This morning at breakfast, to his bewilderment, Potter's plate of bacon and eggs and home fries had formed a smiley face, the crinkly, curled bacon grinning, the yolk eyes gazing, the home fries twisting like the crazy tufts of hair of someone who'd slept poorly, like himself, with a hangover. Potter thought perhaps the kitchen staff had pegged him for a greenhorn, and it was a joke. But perhaps it was an accident, a mere fluke. He looked at Jane's plate, but she was eating waffles. He took his fork and jabbed out the eyes, and cut the grin in half.

The diner was full, but Jane was the only woman, besides the waitress. Groups of local men wandered in and out, clomping around in hip waders and wool shirts, wearing smashed hats with flies hooked in them. They joked freely among themselves, yelling to each other across the room. They all seemed to have secret, familiar destinations along the river, choice fishing spots, but they wouldn't tell anyone outside their party, for fear of being followed. Their women, Potter was sure, were at home, and in revenge he imagined a pleasant horror, these abandoned women scooting through the house in pink, furry slippers and flammable blue nightgowns, frowsy, sad, shapeless, and unloved. He looked down at the broken grin and blinded eyes on his plate, and reconsidered. These men could fish, but he had Jane. He looked up and gave her a warm smile, and shoveled his breakfast away.

Still, he wished he knew about fishing. Potter was intent on it, now that he'd started. He hated incompleteness; for him, it was a matter of policy. Finish what you begin. He needed a fish.

The line tugged sharply and Potter's heart leapt up. He yanked on his pole and reeled in, and as he leaned back, the thin white plastic rod curved into a vicious sickle. It was just a snag. Potter wiggled his pole back and forth, thrashing it furiously and making, by his strenuous efforts, a sort of pantomime of a man who'd hooked a big one, and then his pole straightened, and the line snapped free and fell slack, floating lightly on the surface. He'd lost his fly, but there was one more. He tied it on. The man at the shop taught him how to make the knot. He bit the lead sinker, and drew some slack line, and lowered the fly into the water.

The river crashed and reverberated through the hills. So complete was the sound, it seemed to have no source, coming from everywhere, and filling the world, overwhelming his ears. Potter realized it was the loudness, the amplification that made him feel so small and ridiculous, so precarious; it was the noise that steepened the hills, made them seem as if they were moving, sliding down. He checked to be sure he was centered on his rock. He hoped Jane would come soon.

There'd been a bunch of guys in the cottage next to theirs, and Potter felt they'd been obnoxious and insinuating, even outright lewd, around Jane. They'd get up early and go fishing, and then come back and light a riproaring bonfire, cook some fish, and drink beer all night. One of those nights, Potter saw them burn a chair and a lamp shade from the cottage. They kept inviting Jane over. Potter told her they were hooligans and greasers, and she laughed at him, saying she didn't know what a greaser was, but that they weren't hooligans, they were just guys having fun. "Fun," she had repeated. They're burning perfectly good furniture, he countered. She said, Come on, Potter, we're not in the city anymore. This is nature, the country, she said, just open up and relax, okay? As a sort of conciliatory gesture, to appease Jane and show the neighbors he was a good sport, Potter bought beer and marshmallows and drank with them last night. The guys got a big kick out of the marshmallows, igniting them on sticks and hurling the balls of blue flame into the woods, and Potter got a hangover.

Potter cast across the river, and let the line ride down

the slower current along the far shore. Pulled gently by the current, the submerged fly swung past Potter, and he fed more line out, letting the flow carry it away toward the pool. The sky darkened, and so did the river; the sun was low in the west now, obscured by the mountaintops. His reflection was vague in the pool. All around him, the fall forest closed in, and the cascade of water, the cool, swift, rushing descent upset his balance. Perhaps it was the hangover, but the blend of colors, the wet black bark of firs, the yellow and red leaves waving like hands in the wind, the leaves looping down through the air — these colors in motion rioted vividly in his eyes. It was terrifying to be so alone, misled by his nerves.

He focused on the line. He made his eyes follow the pole out from his hands, and trace the thin lucid thread angling across the water, and sink into the pool where the fly waved gently in the darkness. He trained his sight on the surface where the line disappeared. Just then, he got a strike. He knew it, he felt it immediately. It was alive, it was there, physical and solid. It was a response, a living voice calling out, and he forgot his dread, jerking the pole sharply. In his shock, he yanked too hard, and as he felt the first bite, in that moment he felt the absence, too. The absence vibrated, lingering like a struck note in the air. He reeled in his empty line.

Potter cast again, perfectly, and the line drifted quietly along the dark bank. Excited, he breathed slowly, stilling his breath to nothing as the fly settled in the pool. Again, he traced the curve of the pole, the taut distance of line; he stared at the surface where it sank from sight, trembling slightly, and saw that it set off a succession of faint ripples. Nothing. He hauled the line in, and cast again, precisely as before; he thought if he could only re-create the exact motions, the thrilling note would again sing out, the music would be there, and he would have his fish. He waited for the moment of contact. Nothing again. He cast one final time. Nothing.

Jane was calling to him from the shore. Potter snapped around. He'd been in a trance of sorts, watching his line. He waved to her, and reeled in. The pool was almost black. He'd been on his rock all day, and it now seemed like a long, long time, except for the last moments, which both stood still and passed swiftly in his memory. He splashed across the shallow water and gave Jane a kiss.

"I almost had one," he said.

"Oh, good," Jane said, "then you didn't mind me being gone so long."

"Well, a little bit. I wondered if you'd forgotten."

"Sorry," she said. "I went way past you. I didn't realize it. Was it huge?"

"It was gigantic, I'm sure." In a curious way, Potter felt like he needed the fish to prove that he was happy. "I wish I caught it. It was exciting, it was a complete surprise, just out of nowhere."

They walked up the scrubby trail to the roadside where the car was parked. It was a rented car. It was called a Tempo, and it was a flashy red, like nail polish. "Sexy," the man at the rental place had said. Potter dumped his fishing pole in the backseat. God, he thought, we sure trashed this car up pretty good.

Jane drove. Potter watched the hills roll by. Here and there, they passed quaint little houses, set far back from the road. There was hardly any traffic, and for long stretches they had the road to themselves.

They were still running parallel to the river, bending and turning with it. Groups of men stood alongside the road, packing up, sipping beers. Jane turned on the radio, and flicked the buttons. Potter slouched back in his seat. Almost catching that fish was a feeling too fine to express, he thought. It was very, very exciting; it was so simple, but so exciting. He couldn't get his mind off it.

"God," he said, "it was just, I don't know."

"What?"

"That fish. I think it was the hangover. All of a sudden, I got concentrated."

Potter lit a cigarette, and blew out the smoke, which lingered above his head, briefly, like a bubble of cartoon speech in which nothing was being said. He brushed it away, and cracked the window. Cool fall air rushed through the tiny slit, and sounded like the river.

Jane simply nodded, and shifted in her seat, nudging the gas pedal a little more. Potter watched her — she liked to drive, she had always liked it a lot, and it seemed as though she'd discovered that driving was even more thrilling in a rented car. She was less responsible, she was freer. She drove fast. When she pressed for more gas, the sudden thrust of acceleration forced Potter back into his seat. She tuned in the radio. The signal from some of the Albany stations faded in and out of range as the car snaked back and forth over the winding blacktop.

Potter watched the darkening land go by. Jane turned on the headlights. He had been fishing before — sort of. As a kid, he remembered, he would use his allowance to buy a setup, a short length of line, with sinkers and two hooks and a bobber, and a jar of fluorescent orange salmon eggs at the hardware store, and then he would trudge the mile or two along the clear-cut, where the power lines ran, down to Vitulli's farm. He hadn't thought about that in ages. Vitulli's farm spread across the entire valley, and Potter often went there to play with Joan, a classmate, and climb around the hayloft in the old barn full of gray air and ancient rusting tools and darting swallows. He remembered the chickens were dirty, and the ugly horse frightened him, but the soil, the manure, the straw, and the wide openness of the valley all let loose a pleasant havoc in his mind. His days there were always a rampage of freedom, an escape from the orderly quiet imposed on him at school and at home.

A small creek wound through the farm. It was fairly shallow, and had little blue and yellow footbridges that arched over it at several points along its path. Mrs. Vitulli took old milk canisters, and painted them blue on the yellow bridges, and yellow on the blue, and planted red and purple petunias in them. When he went fishing, Potter always stopped and asked for Mrs. Vitulli's permission as a matter of courtesy, and she always said yes, of course, and gave him a little something, a cookie or an apple to take along. He caught bullhead, mostly. Often Joan would come.

Joan Vitulli's olive skin and almond eyes and sharp

nose were as clear to Potter now as his sensation of excitement was when the fish had struck. He knew what losing the fish felt like now. "I know what it was like," he said. As it grew dark, Potter told the story to Jane, who listened silently.

Joan always wore her hair in a ponytail, knotted with green rubber bands, or bits of yarn, or sometimes clipped back with barrettes or bobby pins. But on one of Potter's visits, she wore it tied with a black velvet ribbon. The ribbon seemed prissy for Joan, who was rough, and something of a tomboy, and Potter told her so. They had slipped between the barbed wire and were walking through the pasture. It was early fall, he remembered, and he heard killdeers crying, and cattails rustled along the creek, and clusters of goldenrod and purple loosestrife bloomed across the field. The grass was dry and flaxen, and when the wind swept across it, shifting patterns of light and dark moved like ocean swells through the field.

The ribbon she wore was so queer, so unusual, Potter made fun of it, and Joan shoved him, and ran away, leaping up to see over the waves of tall grass. Potter chased after her, and finally pulled her down, and they lay together in a bed of trampled grass, silent but breathing so heavily that Potter was embarrassed. It was strange, hearing a girl breathe. They were quiet for some time. Potter remembered listening to the wet sound of their breathing and the wind and the sough like surf rolling over the grass and watching a skein of Canadian honkers wedge through the gray sky above them. It was like being underwater, silent and slow that way. "If you don't like my ribbon, you could take it off," Joan said. Potter didn't say anything, and Joan sat up on her knees, her back facing him. Potter looked at the black ribbon, tied in a bow. "Yeah, go ahead," Joan said. Her hair had shafts of straw sticking to it. Potter reached up and touched the bow. The ribbon was soft and had a smooth gloss, a sort of sheen, when you rubbed it one way, but it was stiff and dull if you rubbed it the other way. His hand skimmed the arrows of feathery, dark hair along the back of her neck as he untied the bow. Her hair fell loose. She shook it free and the straw flew from it and she turned around. "My mother said it would look nice," she said. Potter held the strip of velvet, rubbing his thumb back and forth, feeling first the smooth way, then the stiff way. Then he leaned forward and saw her close her eyes, so he closed his too. Her kiss was the quietest thing in the world. Potter never wanted to open his eyes again, but he did, after a while, and Joan was looking at his face, and smiling. "My sister taught me how in the mirror," she said. Potter couldn't say anything at all. He just leaned forward for more, and he felt the lavender of her lips, and then something else, the moist pink slip of her tongue. He jumped up and started off across the field waving the black velvet ribbon like a flag fluttering in the evening air.

During the chase, sometime before Joan caught and wrestled him to the ground, Potter dropped the ribbon, and though they looked everywhere, trying to be thorough, they never found it. He apologized to Joan over and over as they walked in the falling dark to the warm yellow light of Joan's house. He imagined Mrs. Vitulli would wonder what happened to the ribbon, and he imagined she would find out. He said good-bye to Joan and waited until the door closed. Then he ran back into the field alone and searched for the ribbon until it was too dark to see and far too silent and dark to pretend he wasn't scared. He'd begun to imagine, not a winding black ribbon, but snakes sliding through the dark grass, and he was almost too afraid to move but he forced himself, even though the fear stayed with him as he climbed the clear-cut in absolute darkness, hearing the wires hum. The fear followed him all the way home, as he imagined the lost ribbon lying in the grass.

Potter reached over and squeezed Jane's thigh.

"Do you remember your first kiss?" he asked.

"No," she said. "Not really."

He meant to mock her lightly, but her abruptness surprised him; his sentiments were tuned so differently at the moment.

A few light drops hit the windshield. The wipers turned on, and cut eyelids in the glass. The last light of day silhouetted the mountains. The car leaned smoothly into turns, rocking and twisting and descending. The rain fell harder, and the wipers measured out the time, as Potter imagined again his first kiss, and the falling darkness, and the fear that had tormented him all the way home. In his memory, the fear was gone, or fading away at least. And the fish? What remained was a vibration on the line, a tremor in his hand, a memory of an encounter with nothing, almost, that struck and vanished in a single fused instant, and he played it over and over, listening to it as if it were music. After a while, Jane turned up the volume on the radio, so they couldn't speak.

JANUARY

Snow began falling sometime shortly after midnight, although Potter didn't notice it then, and wouldn't have noticed it now, except that a draft shook the slats of the venetian blind just enough to disturb him. He looked up from a letter he was trying to start. A fringe of mist condensed around the window and the view from his sofa had a soft, bleary focus. He rose, crossed the room, and raised the blind, pressing his face against the glass. Outside, snow slanted past his window, falling in darkness until it was briefly illumined under the cone of blue light from the street lamp. The streets were white and flashing with cold chips of crystal. He hadn't realized snow was predicted. He hadn't realized how late it was, either.

For most of the night, he'd busied himself with listening to an album of baroque Christmas music and working on a letter. In a dreamy and pensive mood, nearly baroque itself, he played the simple variations of Johann Pachelbel's Canon over and over again. The record had belonged to Jane. Wadded balls of pale blue stationery lay on the bare wood floor around the sofa. The letter, to his mother, was not going well. Yesterday had been the Feast of the Epiphany, and it touched off a twinge of nostalgia. He liked to fancy himself a writer, and occasionally he struggled with a script, or wrote an article, but right now he was having a hard time scribbling this simple letter, and in the middle of so many false, fitful starts, he'd craved a baked potato, and two of them were roasting in the oven. "Roasting" was how he thought of the potatoes. Now that he was made aware of the falling snow, the potatoes sounded tastier that way.

Potter lowered the blind. On the white walls of his small apartment there were art prints, most of them left-over from college, all of them nicely framed, although they hung off-kilter, at odd, tortured angles. That was because the apartment itself was composed entirely of skew lines. There wasn't a plumb wall in the place. When Potter first moved in, he noticed he was always leaning his head one way and the other, vaguely searching out true vertical. He never found it. Earlier in the night he'd thought of moving to a better place, but he couldn't imagine where he'd go.

His mother had called the day before to say that she was thinking about him. She wanted to let him know, too, that the Magi had arrived safely in Bethlehem. The journey of the Magi was a drama they played out every year, a routine from his childhood. Potter and his brothers and sisters could watch the Magi wandering through the house and know that Christmas was coming soon. They began their journey on the sill above the kitchen sink and the holiday season was officially finished on the Feast of the Epiphany, when, at last, they made it to the manger, above the fireplace; his mother would arrange a nice supper, and they'd fete the Wise Men, and after that, the vacation was over, and it was time to get on with the business of life. Immediately, his mother would take all the decorations down and throw out the tree. She still did this, even though no one lived at home anymore. He had the image of his mother stealing through the dark, quiet house alone, pushing the Wise Men forward, inch by inch, and day by day.

Potter looked at the letter, a quarter page of black

scrawl that fell to a blank space of blue in midsentence. What was there to say? Christmas morning he opened the package his mother had mailed him, weeks before, thinking it was funny how he'd waited. Because she had sent a present, he'd gone out and bought a small tree to put it under. After he set up the tree he cut snowflakes and pasted loops of green and red construction paper together in a long chain and fashioned a tiny angel out of a rolled cone of purple paper with gold wings stapled to it and a misshapen foil head wedged into the small opening at the tip. The angel he made was a seraphim, with six wings. He taped chocolate Kisses to the tree, for ornaments. In the package from his mother was a gold-plated pen and the pale blue stationery and a card saying Merry Christmas and please write a brief note letting me know how you are.

When the timer rang, he opened the oven door and jabbed his potatoes with a fork. They burned him when he pulled them off with his bare hand, and steam rose in frail curls through the small holes the tines made. He looked through the cabinets, but the last of the foil had gone to make his seraphim. He pulled the angel's head off, and carefully unfolded the balled-up sheet of foil, and wrapped his potatoes. He put on his coat and scarf and black watch cap. He couldn't find his gloves, but it didn't matter. He placed a hot potato in each pocket. At the last minute, on his way out, he grabbed the salt and pepper shakers from his small dining table, shut off the lights, and went down the stairs and into the street for a walk.

The city was empty, as if uninhabited, and yet, as Potter walked, looking into the massed, swirling sky, the whole world was filled with falling snow, and the frantic descent, the crowded way the white flakes flurried as they emerged from the dark sky into the light of the street lamps, made for a fullness which was at odds with the early hour and the cold and the silence. Potter hunched his shoulders against the wind, holding a baked potato in the palm of each of his hands. They were quite hot. He couldn't hold them for long. He let them rest in his pockets until his hands got cold again, and then he held them again.

He walked towards the park. The houses were still dark and quiet and seemed empty, although, here and there, a light glowed through a window and someone's shadow would pass. Snow cut across the warm light like another kind of shadow. Garbage cans lined the streets, and every few houses a Christmas tree lay tipped over, or propped up against an iron gate, often with stray glistening strands of tinsel still hanging from the branches. The deepening snow on the sidewalk drifted smoothly against the garbage cans and boxes of rubbish and flocked the dry, yellowing branches of the trees.

He kicked the untracked snow with his boots, watching the small explosions of powder as he walked on. Under the street lamps, the snow was blue, like diamonds, but in the park, the lamps were different, and the snow glittered like a sea of gold. The lamps in the park were ornamental reproductions of gaslights which burned with a fake yellow flame. The flight of the snow had a golden filigree to it, making a tracery that repeated itself so swiftly and insistently, so perfectly, that it hung suspended and still in the light, as if draped in place.

In the center of the park was a concave band shell. A big star made of white Christmas lights shone brightly above the roof. Garlands of fir wreathed the gutters and red plastic bells swayed soundlessly under the eaves.

Potter didn't see the man until he'd passed him and begun walking toward Main Street. The man leaned over the railing, under cover of the band shell.

"Excuse me? Sir?"

Potter, lost in thought, jerked around. The man came toward him.

"Yes?" said Potter.

"You wouldn't have a light, would you?" the man asked. He was small and fat with thick ears like slices of ham. The hem of his overcoat swept the snow and a frozen rim of ice clung to it. Snow landed on his hatless head and stuck to his hair.

"No, I'm sorry, I don't," said Potter.

The man shivered, and stuffed his hands into his pockets. Through a tangle of trees, beyond the park and across the street, there was a church with sharp spires and a high square bell tower, and a white statue of the Virgin.

The man said, "I don't see what you're doing out here."

"Just walking," Potter said. "I couldn't sleep."

"I was sleeping," said the man, "but now I'm not."

"I wish I had a light for you," Potter said.

Potter sniffed and the air tasted good.

"Is it supposed to snow all night?" he asked.

"I don't know."

"Looks like it. Seems like it might fall all night."

Potter tried to watch the devious path of a solitary flake as it weaved through the branches that arched and twisted above the band shell. It was futile. The flake sailed into the light, and was lost.

"Where do you stay?" Potter asked.

"Here, the mission. Different places."

"Why don't you go to the mission now?"

"I don't like it there all the time," he said. "You pray for everything. You pray for oatmeal."

Potter shrugged.

"I get tired of it."

"Are you hungry?" Potter asked.

"I don't know," he said, "I hadn't thought about it."

"Well?"

"I guess so. I guess I am, if I think about it."

"Would you like a baked potato?"

"Say what?"

"A potato."

"I thought that's what you said. I guess I don't really feel like walking anywhere."

"I've got one right here," said Potter.

Potter pulled one of the baked potatoes out of his pocket. He held the silver ball of foil like a gift he'd produced, magically, out of nowhere. The man stared at the bright wrapping, which sparkled under the fake star's light. Snowflakes dissolved on the hot tinfoil.

"You're shittin' me," he said.

"What else could this be?" Potter asked.

The man thought about it for a moment. "A rock."

"Well, the proof is right here, isn't it? Tell me this isn't a baked potato."

Potter unwrapped the baked potato, and steam rose up through the falling snow.

"This potato is yours if you want."

"What's wrong with it?"

"Nothing. It's just a regular potato. I eat them all the time." Potter reached into his pocket. "Salt and pepper?"

Potter salted the potato lightly, and then doused it in black pepper.

"The salt's for wisdom," said Potter, "and the pepper's so you aren't bored to death. Potatoes can be boring."

Potter watched him as he bit into the potato. "It's hot, Jesus. It's okay, though. It's good."

Potter decided to hold off on his potato. He touched the man's shoulder.

"Enjoy," he said.

"I will," the guy said, swallowing.

Potter walked away and was about at the park's edge when the man yelled. "Hey, my name's John," he screamed.

"I'm Potter," Potter screamed back.

He stopped at a doughnut shop and drank a quick cup of hot chocolate, left a decent tip, and started home. The snow fell even harder now, and it lay thickly over the sidewalks and streets, and covered up the usual litter, and everything was soft and white, with a kind of calm, equable look to it, a stillness and poise, as if all the old lines and divisions had been erased, and a person could start fresh, begin anew. Christmas decorations were still up along Main Street. Big candy canes hung from the street lamps, gaily festooned with green and red streamers, and plastic snowmen in black top hats clung to the poles with one hand, and waved straw brooms high in the air with the other. On every corner, tinny gray speakers crackled and hummed in the cold air, blurting out Christmas carols, like a choir of dime store angels. As Potter crossed an empty intersection, the speaker was singing "Joy to the World." The words drifted in the air and sank like the giddy swoon of angels in flight.

Already, though it was still dark, people had begun to stir, and more lights lit up in the houses along Main Street. Perhaps because of the weather, people were leaving early for work, or perhaps they were always up at this hour. Potter didn't know. He bought a cup of coffee at the all-night deli, thinking maybe John could use some by now. As he was leaving, the Indian man behind the register asked Potter if he would mind doing him a small favor.

"My dear brother is returning to India today," he said, "and we would, please, like to take a photograph. Of me, and my two brothers. We want Mother to see the store. We want her to see how things are with us in America."

"Sure," said Potter, "no problem."

The man waved to his two brothers, and all three came around from behind the counter. The first Indian man had a Polaroid camera. He handed it to Potter.

"Outside," he said.

All of them, including Potter, stepped outside into

the snow. The three brothers stood together on the sidewalk in front of the store. They linked their arms together and flashed broad white grins. Potter futzed with the camera, fumbling for the button. When he looked through the lens, the three brothers shrank, and seemed very far away. He found the button and clicked. The bulb exploded in a burst of blue, and a grinding gear spat out a picture. All of them huddled together, bending their heads to watch it develop, but before it could, through the small opening in their huddle, a snowflake lit precisely where the head of the departing brother would have been. Everything developed, quite slowly in the cold, except this brother's head. There was an eerie white space, an emptiness, where the snowflake fell.

Also, Potter apparently jiggled the camera, and the shot was poorly framed. All the brothers leaned at a funny, seasick angle. They all looked at the photo. They all groaned.

"Let's do it again," said Potter. "That was just practice."

"Yes," said the first Indian, "once more."

"Inside," said the brother whose head had been blotted out. "It's too cold."

Potter imagined that he was sore about the accident to his head. However random and innocent, it must have seemed portentous, like a jinx, on the eve of a long journey. Potter wanted to put him at ease, and devised a brief homily.

"Every snowflake is unique," said Potter. "Like a human being! A soul! Sure, they all look the same when they're falling down, but under closer inspection, under a microscope, you discover this isn't really true. You could consider this accident a good sign, a prophecy, a singular blessing on your trip."

"Yes," said the brother who was leaving. "But you see, I'm freezing my balls off. Inside, hurry."

"No," said the brother who hadn't spoken yet.

The three brothers bunched together again, and flashed broad grins again, and Potter fumbled with the camera, and managed to hold it level, and finally the bulb burst the darkness with a lovely blue explosion, and the gear moaned and gave forth a photograph once more. Potter covered it quickly. When they dared to look, the picture was vague, and still developing, but all the heads seemed to be there, neatly perpendicular, and the picture was going to look right, and everyone was happy.

Even though he went home along the same route, the falling snow had obliterated his tracks, and it was as if he were going a different and entirely new way, as if he had never been there before. When he got to the park, John was gone. Potter hoped he was warm and sleeping safely. He drank John's coffee under the star that sat perched above the band shell. The park was quiet, but when Potter stood inside the band shell, he could hear the ocean, sea surf crashing far away, as if he'd cupped a small shell over his ears. Where the wading pool used to be, two dolphins swam in the sea of gold snow. In the summer, children rode the dolphins, and the dolphins spouted water into the pool. Now, in the snow, they looked like walruses. As he stood there, more and more lights flicked on in the houses surrounding the park. A grayish dawn began to dissolve the dark night, and the gold sea dimmed and faded. When the star flicked off, Potter walked on.

He still held true to his plan, trying to retrace his steps, and still, there was no trace of them. In the distance he thought he heard something like a foghorn keening at regular intervals, but he wasn't sure. For the second time that night he passed Jane's building. He stood on the sidewalk, and stared up at the door. Then he climbed the steps, and rang her bell. He waited.

"Who is it?" he heard through the speaker.

"It's me," Potter announced. "Can I come up?"

There was a silence, and then, farther back within the speaker, he could hear someone else asking, "Who is it?"

There was another silence. Then Jane said, "Tomorrow would be better."

It was precisely what Potter had suspected, and yet he was absolutely surprised. He knew, and he was still stunned.

"Did you lose your key again?" Jane asked.

"No," Potter said.

"What time is it?"

Coming towards him, he heard the loud, rough grinding of a garbage truck, and saw men with big barrels running back and forth in front of the headlights. The headlights cut an intense beam through the murky light. All down the street, as they came closer, Potter saw them hauling Christmas trees to the truck.

He could hear Jane's scratchy voice through the speaker, calling: "Are you there? Hey, are you there?"

Potter listened to the warning blast of the foghorn and watched the garbagemen. They dumped their loads into the truck, flipped a switch, and a motor groaned and the garbage was crushed, and the headlights dimmed under the strain until it was done, and then brightened again. A man in a yellow rubber suit snatched up a nearby tree. Needles shook away as he pitched the dry, dead tree into the truck. Potter watched it crumple and disappear. He was starting to feel cold. The truck and the running men went down the street, farther and farther away, hauling off Christmas trees.

When he got home Potter remembered his baked potato. He pulled it out of his pocket. He also had the Polaroid of the headless Indian. He'd keep it as a souvenir. The picture actually looked like a tableau vivant or one of those antique photo amusements, where a person steps behind a cardboard scene, and pokes his head through a hole, and gets a souvenir snapshot of himself doing something novel and extraordinary. If he could find a small enough picture of himself, he'd cut it out and paste his own head in there. He hoped the Indian had a safe journey. He tacked the Polaroid to the wall. It was hard — no, it was impossible to line up. He stepped back, and looked at it. He shifted it slightly, and stepped back farther, and looked again. If he stared at the square white border that framed the snapshot, the picture was cockeyed, but if he concentrated on the leaning brothers, they seemed as upright and plumb as could be. Was it a perfect picture of leaning brothers, or was it really a slanty picture of normal-standing brothers? Between his two choices, Potter was unable to choose which crooked way was better.

He relit the pilot light on his heater, and turned the gas up high. The blue flames from the heater always mesmerized Potter exactly as if they were a real fire in a fireplace. He put on Pachelbel again and stretched himself out on the sofa. His potato was cold on the outside, but when he cracked it open, it was still hot and steaming in the center. He gave it a light salting and peppered it generously. He was famished. The potato burned his lips, and he slowed down, and when he slowed down, it was good. It was the best, most memorable baked potato he'd ever had. He heaped more black pepper on the last few bites, and ate them, then stared at the blue flames, then out the window.

He got up and turned the Pachelbel over on the turntable. The variations were actually quite monotonous in that fancy, baroque manner, but he sort of liked the monotony, the sameness, the way the canon's variations repeated themselves, wandering, building up, yet always leading back, in the end, to an already familiar place. He turned the volume down. He pulled out the bed beneath his sofa. He slipped off his shoes and his shirt, and pulled off his pants and socks, and quietly set them beside the heater. He turned the gas up a notch so it would be nice and warm when he woke, and then he drew back the top sheet, easing it away gently. He turned off the lights and could again see the snow fall past the window, circling down.

But when the music ended, he was still awake, and

it was too quiet. He put the stationery away and set the cap back on his gold-plated pen. There really wasn't anything to say, at least nothing that couldn't wait until tomorrow, or the day after. Tomorrow, or the day after, he'd remember to tell his mother how apparently other people waited until the Epiphany to throw out their trees, too.

He was a day late. He pulled his seraphim off the small tree and set it aside on the kitchen table. He took the tree over to the window. He raised the blind and opened the window and looked out. The garbagemen hadn't made it to Potter's street yet. Dozens of Christmas trees, propped upright or fallen over, lined the sidewalks. Leaning out the window, Potter thought he heard the foghorn, and he knew he heard something, and it sounded like a cry of warning, of some urgency, but it wasn't a foghorn, he didn't think, because he wasn't anywhere near water. In fact, he was far inland. He looked up and down the street, plucked a last Kiss from the tiny tree, and let it fall.

OPEN HOUSE

THE LAST TIME I'd seen my father he behaved
like one of those wolf-boys, those kids suckled and reared
in the wild by animals, and I was never sure, during the
ten confusing minutes I stood on the lawn outside the
house, whether or not he recognized me. The security
chain on the door remained slotted. Inside, through the
crack, he asked me when I was going to relinquish my
disease, which made me think either he was speaking rhe-
torically or confusing me with my brother Miles, who is
schizophrenic and lives in a halfway. Then he seemed to
have a moment of lucidity and called me a loser for dropping
out of college. He had trouble breathing and rasped and
swore like someone twitched by demons on a downtown
corner. All the flowers, in the hanging baskets, in the clay
pots, in the whiskey barrel, were dead and hissing dryly
in the wind, so it was true, apparently, that he had watered
the garden with gasoline. He gasped, he yelled, he mixed
the latinate with potty talk, calling my sisters complicitous
cunts and my mother a vituperative bitch. His shouting
had always had the effect of diminishing me, the sheer
volume of it taking away the ground I stood on, for it would

sound as if he were screaming across the country or into the past, to someone, at any rate, who was not present, and the longer I remained there, listening, the more invisible I felt. He had a certain emotional vigor that turned his head purple, and all during that most recent visit, his head was purple. When I was a kid he'd put that purple head in my face and grab my jaw and tell me, "If you were me you'd be dead because my father would have killed you." Driving away, I had that feeling, of echoes within echoes.

Certain he was finally and forever crazy, and in need of professional help, I called his shrink, Dr. Headberry, but that poor, harassed pill dispenser had been fired, or dismissed, and then, about a week later, my father tried to take his suffering public. He came to church dressed in his version of sackcloth and ashes — tin pants, snake boots, a wool coat with suede ovals at the elbows, and a plaid cap with foam earflaps. These things had long ago been banished to hooks in the garage, and smelled, I knew, of motor oil and grass clippings and the dusty, forgotten odor of fabrics that have gone damp and dried, then gone damp again and dried again, endlessly over the years. He'd locked away his guns after my brother Jackie (as my father liked to say) sucked a barrel — shoved a twelve-gauge Mossberg back in his tonsil area and opened his skull against the bedroom wall.

While both my older brothers were evidently fucked up, I, as the baby of the family, was luckily buffered by my four sisters. If it wasn't for them, I knew I'd be way more of a mental clodhopper than I was, or dead or crazy. Karen, Lucy, Meg, and especially Roxy, they all had this special way, this oddball interest in good places to paddle canoes, and herb remedies, and parks where you could take safe walks in the dark, and sardonyx and black fire opals, and weird healing practices, and crow feathers and chips of eggshells, and numerology, and playing records backward, and food that didn't come out of a can or box. My father thought they were witches. Roxy carried a bull thistle in a tea infuser chained around her neck. The Salish Indians believed thistles would ward off bad luck, and the Scots believed they would keep away the enemy. Roxy gave me a thistle of my own and once she gave me a pomegranate. I'd never seen one before, and I was surprised that someone could think of me, sitting downstairs in Jackie's room, on Jackie's old bed, and bring me a gift out of nowhere, and for no reason. A pomegranate. *Out of nowhere, and for no reason!* Isn't it perfect, she asked, and it was.

I watched my father from across the aisle. He knelt in a pew with his head bowed and his hands hung limply over the backrest as though he'd been clamped into a pillory. Lawyers for both sides had called me, asking if I'd testify if the divorce went to trial, but I had no idea what I'd say if I were being deposed. He looked drunk and sleepy and wired, and also penitent in this odd, remembered way, as if he were still trying to fool some buzzard-backed nun from his childhood. He wiped sweat from his brow with a wrinkled hankie, mopped the back of his neck, held the thing like a flag of truce as he folded his hands for prayer. During the Offertory he began crying or weeping — weeping, I guess, because there was something stagey about it. He beat the butt of his palm against his head, lifted his eyes to the Cross, and said, "Oh God, oh God, my God."

"I wish I could be crucified," my father had told me over the phone, the day after he was served papers. "That's really the only way to settle these things."

Despite the lunacy of pitting his agony against the agony of Jesus Christ, I now decided he wasn't crazy. This was calculated. He'd come to menace and harass my mother. For years church had been her only bastion and retreat and he'd come as a trespasser to violate it, to pollute its purity and calm, to take it away from her, and make it ugly like everything else in our life, and that's what I'd tell the lawyers. I was no disciple or defender of the church and no big fan of the snobs who weekly attended Mass. With its pale green walls and polished pine benches and high windows of distorted glass it seemed a place for lame rummage sales, a place where fussy old men sold boxes of yesterday's best-sellers, soup ladles, and wide neckties. The young seemed old, and the old seemed ancient — widowers in pleated pants who had retired into a sallow golden age, bereft men with nothing to do but sip their pensions like weak tea in a waiting room whose only door opened on death. And the women — some so fanatically dedicated to a pre–Vatican II universe they still wore hats within the nave, and if they'd forgotten a scarf or hat, they'd unclasp their purses and find a Kleenex and bobby-pin that to their hair. Arranged in the pews, these solemn women with toilet paper pinned to their heads looked like planted rows of petunias. Yet that Saturday, as my father crudely interrupted the service, I considered the possibility that the heart and soul of any faith is absurdity, and that these ridiculous, otherworldly women, with their silly gestures, might just be saints.

The Mass stopped and everyone turned from the altar and stared at him. Everyone — the Greys, the Hams, the Wooleys, Mrs. Kayhew and the Grands and the Stones, etc. Also the priest, the altar boys. It was a caesura that filled with whisperings of disbelief and doubt, and only my mother, who was the Eucharistic minister and sat in the sanctuary, remained quiet and calm. She laced her hands together and buried them like a dead bird in her lap. Sitting in her chair, icily withdrawn, she looked as she did when I was a child and dinner was not going well, evenings when my father occupied the head of the table like a cigar store Indian and silence settled in our bones and we could hear little else but the tink-tink of fork tines and the sound of chewing and it was painful to swallow. Those nights I wouldn't eat the hard things, the raw carrots or bread sticks, for fear of making a noise, and my mother wouldn't eat at all. My mother liked to say that silence had made her a very slender woman, and it was true, she was slim and at sixty still looked girlish in blue jeans.

The priest drank wine from the chalice and, wiping the rim, held the cup to my mother's lips. He leaned toward her, whispered something in her ear, and she shook her head deliberately. Together they stepped down to the Communion rail. My father waited until the line dwindled down, then lifted himself awkwardly, stumbling up the aisle alone. I saw Mrs. Grand lay a hand on her husband, restraining him. My father stood, swaying a little, before my mother. Later, after my mother returned from her trip to Texas, she would tell me it was not her place to judge, and certainly not her role as the morning's Eucharistic minister. Her faith gave her the ability not to judge anything, even movies. To me, as an outsider, and someone without any faith at all, the scene at the Communion rail seemed a show of profound strength, but my father, later, would say he only went up there to prove what a chickenshit she was. The church was dead quiet. My mother lifted the Eucharist as you would a bright, promised coin, holding it slightly above eye level, and my father looked up. "Body and Blood of Christ," she said, and he responded, "Amen," and then she very carefully set the host on his waiting tongue.

After the blessing my mother left the sanctuary and knelt in the front pew. The door in the vestibule had been jammed open with a rubber wedge and a cool wet wind circulated through church, stirring the lace edge of the altar cloth and the sprigs of white gladiolas in their fluted gold standards. Her friends filed out, and cars left the lot. She remained kneeling on the padded hassock and prayed with her eyes shut and with her eyes shut she heard, from the vestibule, the ruffle of the priest's soutane as the black skirt swept the floor, and then the hurried, plodding steps of my father. She remained still and continued to pray.

"She denied me and she denied me," my father said to the priest. "She denied me even the simplest things a husband requires."

The priest gestured helplessly toward the confessionals — the penalty boxes, my father called them, those two upright coffins in the corner of the church. Probably it crossed the priest's mind that the formality of this arrangement might help contain my father's apparent madness. A closed door, at the very least, might muffle his complaint. My father didn't often go out in public because he thought people didn't like him, and when he did socialize, out of nervousness and excessive drinking, he was a terrible gasbag, and most people did try to avoid him, and so the fact that he'd come to church, and made such an awful ruckus, now swayed me back in the direction of the idea that he must be crazy. I was about to step in, but the priest waved me away.

"Even bedtime pleasures."

The priest said, "I'm sure there's more to the story."

"Don't tell me about stories," my father responded. "Calumny is one of the seven deadly sins."

"No it isn't," the priest said, firmly.

My father ignored him, shouting at my mother.

"How dare you judge me! You call yourself Christians!"

The altar boy returned to snuff the candles and collect the cruets of wine and water. My mother could smell the curls of black smoke rising from the burnt wicks. With her eyes closed, she felt as though she could lift herself up, she could rise away and soar, as she said her prayers, on the whispered fluttering wing beat of words, away, away, away . . . while my father stared after her from what then seemed a lifetime of hatred. She did not move. Her skin was pale to the point of appearing blue. Her fingers, interlaced, were delicate and weak. She was as still in her pew as the pale crucified Christ floating high above the sanctuary, but she was gone.

"Goddamn you to hell," my father screamed on his way out the door.

I hadn't dropped out of school. In early March the bursar asked me to withdraw until the outstanding balance on my tuition bill was paid. I stuffed a rucksack with clothes and left campus that night. I was relieved. My lisp made me quiet and shy, embarrassed at the sound of myself, and also something of a hostile shit. People gathered in their dorms, smoked bong hits under batik bedspreads that breathed, and endlessly analyzed their families. I couldn't do it. The soft sibilance of my voice didn't square with what I had to say, and I felt paralyzed by a pressure, a sense that if I started talking there was a good chance I'd never stop. To cure this, or get around it, I had signed up for a writing course, but dropped it when I couldn't figure out the economy of a story, the lifeboat ethics of it — who got pitched in with the sharks, who got rescued. By the end of January I had stopped attending classes, and only turned in the written assignments, and sometime in February I pulled the curtains and lay in bed for a week.

I left school without telling anyone, in part because as a rule, a policy, I never say good-bye. The night I walked off campus was quiet, I remember, that country quiet where every sound seems to have a distinct place in the world, as arranged as notes in a Bach sonata, and by the next morning I'd hitched to Altoona, Wisconsin. From there I hopped a freight train home to Seattle. Twice as the train crossed trestles over the Yellowstone and then later over the Clark Fork I considered jumping off to do some fishing, but the divorce was already in progress and I was convinced my father was going to destroy the contents of our house. (He did: he burned the christening dress we'd been baptized in, he tossed our photo albums, etc.) Back in Seattle I rented a shoe box room and got a job busing tables at a restaurant owned by two lesbians I knew from day one would eventually fire me. (They did.) I spent most nights hunched over my vice, drinking beer and tying flies, filling one box with hare's ears and pheasant tails, and another with size 16 Blue-winged Olives and Pale Morning Duns. My only plan in the world right then was to hop a train to Livingston, hitch into the park, and fish the Firehole near the west end of Fountain Flats, a place that was a favorite of both Miles and Jackie. After that, after Memorial Day, I planned to take my tent and stove and live in the park all season. (Which I did, until I woke one morning with my tent sagging like a collapsed parachute and was driven out by snow in mid-October.)

The only things I wanted out of our house were Miles's old fly rod and the original fifteen and a half pages of Jackie's suicide note.

Realtor's signs had been staked into the front and side yards, and a sandwich board stood spraddled on the sidewalk. "Open House," it said, "Sunday," and the lead agent's name was Cynthia. My father's beat spy car was parked in the drive, the passenger door lashed shut with loops of clothesline, the landau top half-scalped, peeling back to raw metal. For weeks he'd been tailing my mother around town in this battered, rust-bitten Plymouth. Was this corny or dangerous? In the last days, as the end drew near, he'd thrown her down the stairs, grated her arm with a grapefruit knife — but the end had been drawing near regularly for twenty years, my entire life, and the tragic end of it all was the very rhythm of our hearts, and if two of my sisters, Roxy and Karen, hadn't finally abducted my mother, hadn't dragged her out of the house, she would have stayed, I bet, and would still be getting chased around the house with knives and screamed at.

I was the youngest of seven children, and my family's history had always been my future, a past I was growing into and inheriting, a finished world, a place where the choices had been made, irrevocably. As a result I was never very interested in the riddle of heredity or the way dysteleology can become design. I arrived too late to believe any other world existed. I was fourteen when Miles started living either on Western Avenue behind the Skyway coat factory or at the VA or in a series of ratty halfway houses, and by now I just assumed the voices Miles heard would speak to me also. I was sixteen when Jackie killed himself. At twenty, I assumed madness would visit me, and so would suicide. I assumed they would approach quietly and hold out their hands and claim me and take me where they had taken my brothers. Miles had tried to kill himself too, driven by his voices to jump off the Aurora Bridge, but he'd survived. Frequently, obsessively, I fantasized sitting on the bridge railing and shooting myself in the head. That way in one moment I'd bring my brothers together in me.

I was convinced I'd know them in that way. And my father? Would I know him? Could I even describe him? Often my father couldn't take a shit unless my mother held his hand. But I couldn't really imagine that.

I looked up, and there he was, framed in the open window of Miles's old bedroom.

"You can't come in," he shouted. "My lawyer guy said nobody can come in the house. Not you, not anybody. I'm sorry, I know it sounds stupid, but too many negative things redound in my direction."

"I came to get my stuff," I said.

"I have to insulate me totally."

He disappeared from the window and reappeared at the back door. He opened it a crack, steel chain still slotted.

"We did this last week," I said.

"You can't come in. I'm sorry, too many negative things. You're all complicitous with your mother. I didn't want this. It wasn't my idea. I wanted to work it out. There's family solutions to family problems, but this, this is appalling and obscene, it's immoral."

"I have a key," I said.

"Not anymore you don't. I changed the locks."

The back porch was lined with clay pots full of dead marigolds, woolly brown swabs on black stalks.

"What's wrong?" I asked.

"Wrong? Nothing's wrong except your mother's got me by the fucking balls. She's got her hooks in me but I'm fine."

I picked up one of the clay pots and put my nose to the soil and it had the cold smell of gasoline.

"Did you pour gas on the flowers?"

"That's just more of your mother's calumny."

"I think we should call Dr. Headberry," I said.

"Headberry? I just talked with him. Headberry says I have no real problems. He's got your mother analyzed perfectly, though. It's ugly. She's got control of my life."

He was lying about Headberry, of course, and unless something happened we were going to continue having the kind of conversation that you have when there's only one seat left on the bus.

"Let me in."

"I don't understand the ugliness — the enormity of the entire process. So many hooks there — they've got control of my life."

I dropped the pot, letting it shatter on the porch, and started walking back out to my truck.

"This is against my better instinct," my father said. He closed the door and slipped the chain off. "It's against everything I know and against my lawyer's advice too."

"Thanks," I said. I nodded out toward the Realtor's sign. "There's an open house tomorrow."

"Yeah, yeah," he said. "Well, I guess you're here and you're coming in and we'll talk and maybe have a drink and then you'll leave. So let's start. Come on in."

Except for boxers drooping off his ass, he was naked. His hunting outfit was piled on a shelf in the kitchen.

He shook his head, and scratched the thick, knotted hair on his chest, then rubbed his arms, his stubbled face.

"Feel like my veins are turning into worms," he said.

"Why'd you come to church?"

"Hey, don't forget I let you in," he said. He grabbed his coat off the shelf and pulled a piece of paper out of the pocket. "I got the restraining order right here. I take it with me everywhere I go. I felt the need to talk to a priest." He scratched the pale insides of his arm, and examined the legal document. "I don't think the law applies to a church," he said. "Once you get inside you have asylum."

He returned the paper to his coat pocket and then picked up the kitchen garbage can, reached his hand in, and pushed aside newspapers, a tuna can, a melon rind.

"See?" he said.

He meant to show me a prescription bottle at the bottom of the can. I lifted it out, gave it a rattle, and held it to the light.

"There's one left," I said.

"I quit," he said. "Thirty-five years and now I've kicked 'em cold turkey."

My father never talked about his own father, and the oldest story he ever told me about himself was of the way snow whipped off Lake Erie in August of 1953, great blinding gusts and rolling drifts, the summer landscape sculpted into a sea of white. Fantastic! A miracle! Naturally, of course, it hadn't been August. He'd been hospitalized, locked up in a Cleveland sanatorium and then shocked out of his mind for six months, and the snow was falling in January, the day of his release. Why, in telling me this, had he left the story in its state of confusion? Now I thought of the snow in August. At the time electroconvulsive therapy was an experimental procedure and current thinking called for barbiturates in long-term intractable cases. That, then, was science and the bold sci-fi future. My father, the day of his release, filled his prescription at a corner druggist and renewed it regularly, like his subscription to the *Wall Street Journal,* for the next thirty-five years.

"When d'you quit?"

"It's a booger, man," he said, clawing at his arms and again at the matted hair on his chest. "I tried watching TV. Then I tried taking a shower and banging my head against the wall."

"You just now tossed these," I said.

"Why the fuck do you think I'm traipsing around the house naked?" he shouted. "My clothes were driving me crazy, that's why."

"I'd like to call Headberry."

He scratched himself some more. "Worms, man. I feel like I could explode. You want a drink?"

The gin and limes and a tray of melting ice were already out on the sink counter. He fixed us two drinks and we sat at the dining table. Across the street the Grand and Wooley families walked out onto their adjoining lawns. A badminton net was strung across the property line on metal stakes. The kids, some of them my age, stood on one side, and the parents stood on the other. Everybody carried rackets and Mr. Wooley, in chinos and a pink shirt, opened a canister of birdies. Bill Grand said something and Bill Wooley leaned back and aimed a silent laugh at the sky.

"I hate those redundant bastards," my father commented.

"You don't even know them."

"Sure I do, you know one, you know 'em all." He

sipped his drink with fine relish. "Where's your mother going?"

It surprised me that he knew she was going anywhere, and I was caught off guard.

"I'm not saying," I said, and now there was a secret between us.

"She's having an affair."

"Mom? Mom's not having an affair."

"What makes you so sure?"

"Who with, then?"

My father looked away, out the window. "Jesus Christ, probably." He sucked an ice cube out of his drink and bit it, spitting glassy splinters. "She's got me by the nuts."

"Hardly," I said. "You're free."

"Free? Free my ass. You know, I've never been to the rain forest — isn't that a phenomena? She's mortgaged my work effort."

For the longest time I thought this was an old bromide all fathers told their kids. Don't mortgage my work effort. No one in this house is going to mortgage my work effort. Roxy took me to the dictionary and explained. *Mort,* she said, means dead. And *gage,* she said, means security.

"That doesn't make any sense," I told him now.

"No? Okay, fine. What's up with you?"

I guessed we were going to ignore the scene at church. Somehow we had agreed to forget it.

"I had a dream about you last night."

"Other people's dreams are boring."

"I was over here, in the kitchen. You were trying to

give me some medicine, like when I was a kid, with a squeeze dropper. Like liquid aspirin. But I wasn't a kid anymore. You were holding the back of my head and telling me to open my mouth. 'Open up,' you said, and when I did, you put a gun in my mouth and kept saying, 'Thataboy, take your medicine. Take your medicine, you'll feel better.' "

"Goddamnit," he said.

"It's just a dream."

"Let's talk about something else. You hear the latest about Mr. Kayhew?"

"No, what?"

"You knew a blood vessel popped in his head? Up in an airplane, up there behind the curtain, first class, knowing the Kayhews. He wasn't dead, just in a coma. I heard they rented him his own apartment and he lived there in a coma."

"I didn't know."

"I'm practically there myself."

I must have made a face.

"What? I'm serious. When I die I'll be exploded to shit. People'll look in the box and say, 'Good God, what the hell killed him?' "

My dad sipped his drink again, keeping an eye on me over the lip of his glass.

"Just everything," he said, answering himself. "Anyway, Kayhew's out."

"Out?"

"He was in a coma."

"You told me that," I said. "So he's out of it now?"

"I guess. I guess you could say that. He's dead."

"That's not what people usually mean when they say someone comes out of a coma."

"Well, it's a little-discussed medical fact, but dying is the other way out."

After a moment, he said, "We were friends, you know, me and Kayhew. Not great friends, but I liked him all right and he liked me. I think he liked me. He never actually said he liked me, but anyway, the point is, I read his obit — he was much beloved, survived by, all that phoney baloney — and he was only sixty-five years old. Sixty-five. That's six years older than me. You know how many days that is?"

"Do you?" I said.

"Two thousand one hundred and ninety," my father said. "Given my habits, I figure I've got two thousand days left." He raised his eyebrows. "This is one of them." He shrugged. "How's your drink? You want another? I'm having another."

"I'll hold off," I said.

But he made me a drink anyway. When he returned to the table, a cigarette dangled from his lips.

"Smoking?"

"Two thousand days, man. Who gives a crap?"

I left the split seeds and floating pulp of my old drink and started the new one. I held the glass to the light and the fresh gin at that moment seemed to be the clearest thing I'd ever seen in my life.

"Miles used to say certain streams were gin clear," I said. "That's how he'd describe them."

"I hate fishing."

"I was only remembering. It was just something to say."

"I've worked in insurance all my life," he said. "The actuarial tables are incredibly accurate. They'll nail you to the wall just about every time. You can read those things and then call a mortician and make an appointment. Like Jackie."

Jackie's last day, his last hour, was an obsessive concern of mine. I'd reconstructed it. I knew where he went, who he talked to, the last tape he played in his stereo ("Johnny Was," by Stiff Little Fingers). The night Jackie shot himself my mother had come into his bedroom. He was at his desk, writing. It was shortly after eight-thirty. He wore a green and gray flannel shirt, blue jeans with blown-out knees, black army boots. Jackie wouldn't turn around and face her. She went back upstairs to tell my father something was strange, that Jackie had a shotgun in his room. "I'm watching a TV show," he said, "don't interrupt me. And close the door when you leave." But that doesn't really explain. What he told my mother that night he told her every night. Without the punctuation of Jackie's death the night of November twenty-sixth, and all the information I'd gathered about it, would mean nothing. But at four-thirty in the morning when the police lights pulsed in the graying air and a couple cops stood on the lawn discussing the case I ran out there in my pj's. "It wasn't suicide," I screamed at them. "It was murder!"

"You want a smoke?" My dad waved his pack of Pall

Malls at me. He went to the kitchen and fished in the garbage can and set the tuna can between us. "No ashtrays. I quit these buggers to save money. I calculated it out that I was spending two hundred bucks a year on cigs. That was when I only made two hundred a month. A whole month's salary. So I quit."

"Where's the rug?" I asked.

I had just felt with my feet below the dining table that the oriental rug wasn't there.

"What? The rug, I don't know."

"That's weird," I said. "All my life it was under the table and now it's gone."

"Crazy, huh?"

I finished my drink, stood, and said, "I'm gonna split. First I want to get some stuff."

"Stay here," my dad said. "I can't have you running around the house."

"It's my house too."

"On what piece of paper does it say this is your house?"

"There's only two things I want."

"Look, sit down. Okay? Sit down. Let's have another drink."

"I want Miles's fly rod. You don't fish and I want it."

"It's yours, you can have it. Okay? Jesus. I hate fishing. Fishing makes me feel fucking hopeless."

"And the christening dress, I want that too."

"I'm not sure where that is," my dad said.

"Crazy, huh?"

"Yeah, it's fucking nuts."

Out the window the Grands and Wooleys were playing badminton in the lowering light. I could faintly hear their shouts and cries as they chased the birdie. The gray air seemed to be filling the house like rising water.

My dad said, "It's wild."

I waited for him to say what was wild, but he only looked out the window.

"What?"

"I can't make the data stand still."

My father sipped his drink meditatively and watched.

"So what's your mother doing in Texas?" he asked.

"How do you know she's going to Texas?"

"She went to the travel agent. She used our credit card to charge the ticket. That's how."

"You put on quite a show at church this morning."

"A show?"

I was starting to feel hazy, blurred. "Yeah, a show. You almost looked like somebody in need of pity."

I shook a Pall Mall from the pack, lit it. My dad watched the badminton game wind down. The Wooleys and the Grands seemed to be running around their lawn swatting flies. Cheers went up, moans, cries, but I could no longer see what they were chasing. It was too dark. A clock ticked in the living room and the refrigerator buzzed and a wind must have risen because behind me a branch scratched the window. A car turned the corner.

"I'll get that stuff," I said.

"You know what the agent told me? Cynthia — that's her name, Cynthia — she told me the place had bad vibes."

"I don't get it."

"We'll have to sell below the appraised value," my dad said. "We won't get near the asking price. They all know Jackie killed himself in the basement, they know Miles is crazy, they know all that shit."

"They? Who's they?"

"People." He looked at me. He smiled grimly. "Do what you have to do. I'm having another drink. This gin is something, huh?"

Our basement was a museum housing a collection of all the usual artifacts. In bins and racks, we had baseball bats, broken skis, tennis rackets with warped guts, wingless gliders, golf clubs, aquariums, hula hoops, a bowling ball, and several orange life jackets my dad had purchased at a lawn sale, along with an old O'Brien water ski and a gas can, all with the idea, a very sudden, impulsive idea, that he'd buy a boat, too. For weeks after we saw boats gleaming in showrooms or parked on trailers in someone's driveway or heading out to sea or docked at a slip in the Union Bay Marina. I don't know what happened to that idea, but here were four faded life jackets, hooked on tenpenny nails. Along a rickety wooden shelf were cases of canned peas and corn and thirty-weight oil, a box of powdered milk, several bottles of novitiate wine — bulk items of a big family. In boxes were tools, tools to fix everything, from loose chair legs to leaky faucets. C-clamps, crimpers, a circular saw. With a tool in his hand, my dad was no better than a caveman. He couldn't fix anything. He usually ended up clubbing whatever wouldn't work, breaking it worse. But he loved tools, he strolled through hardware stores handling trouble lights and blue hacksaw blades with the enthusiasm other people might reserve for the Louvre.

I found what I was looking for: a polished cherry wood case, narrow and about two and half feet long. I brought it upstairs and turned on a light. I popped the hasp, and opened the box. The inside was lined with crushed velvet, and hand-carved bridges at either end held the rod in place. I lifted the butt end out, cradled the sanded cork in my hand. The cane was pale blond, unmarred by knots or coarse grain, and the lacquer, gin clear, seemed only to draw out the bamboo's simplicity; the reel seat was rosewood, the fittings nickel-plated; the guides gleamed; the ferrules were wrapped in blue and green thread, winding in a spiral pattern. I heard the ice in my dad's glass clink, and then he was there, looking at the rod over my shoulder. I turned the rod in my hand. Miles had called the whole family down to his workbench in the basement the day he signed it. He used a Chinese brush from which he'd clipped all but a single horsehair. I remember watching him do it, the way he held one hand steady with the other while, miraculously, his name looped across the cane in a single stroke.

"That's art. That's a piece of work," I said.

"Not bad for a crazy fuck," my dad said.

"He wasn't crazy then." I angled the rod in the light. "It's just the opposite of how he is now. It's simple."

"Have another drink?"

"No," I said.

From the kitchen, Dad said, "You planning a trip?"

"Wyoming," I said. "I'm gonna live in the park all season."

"That's stupid," Dad said. "Here's your gin."

"I said no. What's stupid about it? I go there every year."

"What about school?"

"What about it?"

"Don't look at me that way," my father said. "I'm broke."

"Anyway, it's where I tossed Jackie's ashes," I said. After he'd been cremated, we were each given an envelope of ashes, just a pinch — you'd throw more oregano in a pot of spaghetti sauce.

"Where?"

"Well, you've never been there, so it's hard to describe."

"Hey, guy, it's good to see you."

"You're drunk."

"I don't think I've talked to anyone for ten days, two weeks."

"You're talking pretty good tonight."

"I guess I am. Imagine if you were God and had to listen to all this."

And then I must have said yes. I should have gone back to the shoe box, and there were four or five opportunities to say no, no, I've had enough, I got what I wanted, see you. But the evening kept opening up, wider and wider, accepting every vague word and half-assed idea. Everything was finding a place; there was a room at every inn. The night became like a fairy tale in which every juncture is answered with a yes and the children hold hands and merrily march down the dark trail into a furnace. The gin ran clear, the tuna can was full of stubbed Pall Malls, I was drunk and awake and my dad was drunk and awake, and the space was there, yawning, and something had to happen.

"Tell me where your mother is?" Dad was saying.

"No way," I insisted.

"Tell me."

"Okay," I said. I squinted a teasing look across the table. "I'll trade you."

"You already got the fly rod."

"I want the original of Jackie's letter."

"Can't do it. I don't know where it is."

"Oh well —"

"All right."

"Get it," I said.

"You don't trust me?"

"Oh, I don't think so."

When he brought the letter back I checked to make sure all fifteen and a half pages were there, licking my fingers and counting them like bills.

Then I said, "She's gone to see an angel."

"An angel, huh?"

"In the bark of a tree, a cottonwood. In the middle of a junkyard somewhere in Texas. There's been reports, so she's going to see for herself."

"It's been in the papers. I've read about that angel." He lit a cigarette, waved the smoke from his face. "Hey, we got coffee stains in the carpet look like angels. We got angels in this house."

A bus passed out front. An old habit, I looked through the window to see if any of my brothers and sisters were coming home.

"Your mother was never anything but a whore. She got me fired off my job. All slander."

"The reason you were fired is because no one likes you. You're an asshole — that's actually a quote."

"Who said that? Markula?"

"I'm not telling."

"I got something else to give you," my father said.

He disappeared again and when he returned to the table he set the shotgun and a box of shells in front of me.

I said, "That's the gun."

"Cops took this as evidence," my father said. "Suicide's a crime. Evidence? Heigh-ho — but I got it back."

In the garage we gathered up gunnysacks, some twine, and a flashlight, and loaded everything into the Plymouth.

"Me and Miles used to do this," my dad said, as we drove away.

"I'm not too big on guns," I said.

"Neither was Jackie. You took after him on that."

"I hope not."

"A gun doesn't mean anything."

"Huh?"

"Take a caveman," my father said. "You put a short arm of some sort, a .38 or what have you, you put it on the ground with some other stuff, like a rock and a sewing

machine and a banana. Ordinary things. What's the caveman going to do? Huh? He's not going to look at the banana
and think, oh, this'd be good on cornflakes. He's not going
to take the sewing machine and stitch up a tutu. And he's
not going to look at the gun and think, maybe I'll blow my
head off. You see what I'm saying."

I thought I did, and then I was sure I didn't.

"I'm nearly broke," my dad said.

"No you're not."

"I thought I'd be living with more dignity by this time,
but it's not turning out that way."

"You're lying," I said. It wasn't an accusation, more
like a statement. We were stopped at a four-way intersection. My father steadied his hands by curling them tightly
around the wheel.

"Maybe I should do the Jackie thing," he said.

"Fuck you," I said. The words just popped out of my
mouth, like a champagne cork. Now my hands were trembling and I put them in my coat pocket. "Don't ever say
that again."

"Why are you so pissed all of a sudden?"

"Let's just go. Let's get those birds."

I've read and reread Jackie's letter to us, I've searched
the final paragraph for a summation. Now I had the original. The letter is long. In it he lists the things he likes:
wolves and trains, the Skagit River, coasting a bike down
Market Street to Ballard. He talks about my mom, dad,
my four sisters, and Miles, but at no time does he mention
me. Toward the last few pages I sense a creepy mortmain,
as if my father's hand is folded over his, guiding the pen

across the page, line by line. Is he trying to say something about himself, or about my father? The letter goes on for fifteen and a half long, tightly scrawled pages, but I'm drawn to the end, even though I know the outcome. I look at the last word and think of the moment when he put down the pen and picked up the gun and pulled the trigger. How much time passed? Had he been thinking it over? To pull the trigger he would have used the same finger he used to press the pen against the paper. What went on in that space? Between the pen and the gun?

Under the freeway we found a cement ledge. A sleepy cooing came from the recess, the occasional flutter of beating wings. It sounded like a nursery at naptime.

"You stay down here," Dad said. "I'll hand the birds to you."

He chinned himself onto the ledge, grunting loudly. He wiped shit off his hands and I passed him the flashlight. He aimed the beam at the birds, a row of them squatting along the ledge. The first bird was mottled gray and brown with beady eyes like drops of melted chocolate. Its eyes remained wide open, stunned and tranced, staring into the beam, unable to move or turn away from the white light. Dad stroked the bird's throat gently. "Come to Papa," he said, and when he'd soothed it somewhat he grabbed it by the neck and passed it down to me. I could feel its heart beating in my hand. I slipped the bird into the gunnysack. The pigeon flopped around, trying to orient itself. Dad jacklit another and another. Some were white as doves, others black as crows. After we'd bagged five birds I tied off the first sack with twine and started a new one. Dad handed me five more paralyzed pigeons and then jumped down.

"That ought to do it," he said. He brushed molted gray feathers from his face, from his arms. "Look at that," he said.

The sacks were alive with confused pigeons, two blobs rolling down the hill. You could see the birds struggling to take off, stupidly beating against the burlap. We ran after them, two drunks at a pigeon rodeo, each grabbing a sack.

We put the birds in the backseat of the car. I picked a downy feather from my father's ear.

"You still pissed?" he said.

"Don't make hollow threats."

"You think it was hollow?"

"I've heard it before."

"Feel like it was just yesterday I was driving around the woods with the Beauty Queen, trying to get my hand up her skirt."

My father laughed. The Beauty Queen was my mother. She'd been Miss Spanaway in 1954.

"Well," he said, gesturing broadly with a sweep of the bottle, "I did. Seven kids. One dead, one crazy. Four girls who don't want a damn thing to do with me. Then you. What the fuck's wrong with you, I wonder?"

"We going?"

The pigeons were insane, jumping around inside the sacks. A crazy burlap aviary. My father got out of the car, took the sacks, and spun the birds in circles. When he put them back in the seat, they were quiet.

"You're the only one left. You'll bury me," my father said. "You'll have to write my obituary."

Generally my father was what people call a paper killer. He drove to a firing range and clamped on ear protection and stood in a port lined with blue baffle shield and shot two-bit targets. Bull's-eyes, black silhouettes, now and then the joke target of a dictator's face in profile. At the end of an afternoon of shooting, he'd roll up and rubber-band his targets, tacking the best to a wall in his den, like trophies. "You shoot against your old self," he'd told me. Of the boys, it was my crazy brother Miles who enjoyed guns. Jackie hated them. The first and only time he'd ever fired a gun the barrel was in his mouth. Obviously, you don't need to be a sharpshooter to kill yourself. Even before Jackie, I'd never liked guns. My father sensed this hesitance, and took me out to the woods, trying to teach me to see things and then trying to get me to shoot them out of the trees. Squirrels, robins. The only time I'd actually fired a gun with him was at a gravel pit. He stood behind me and watched as I leveled his bolt-action .22 at a row of pop cans. He calmly gave me directions, but I quickly aimed high and pinched off a round, missing, then chambering another round and missing again, spent shells skittering at my feet in brassy flashes, until I dry-fired and knew the gun was empty. I was ten years old and it was the first time I'd ever felt like I was not in control of myself. I'd been feeling the urge to turn around and shoot my father.

It was near dawn when we parked at the gravel pit. I hadn't been there in ten years and it was now abandoned, a maze of packed dirt roads, each ending in a cul-de-sac of bitten earth. I carried the pigeons and the gin and Dad carried the gun. The sky was just beginning to pale with a metallic dawn light outlining a dark fringe of trees. We sat down.

"Can't drink like I used to," Dad said.

I raised an eyebrow. "How'd you use to?"

"I didn't mean I don't drink like I used to," he said. "Just I can't." He coughed up a laugh, breathing in short, swift rasps. He lit a cigarette. "My lawyer call you?"

"He did."

"You gonna testify?"

I thought about it, briefly, as shapes in the gravel pit took on solidity. People were using it as a dump. Washing machines, the odd chair, boxes and lawn bags, bent and twisted gutters, a suitcase.

"I wouldn't let it go to trial," I said.

"You mean I don't have a chance?"

I imagined my father's life caught up in the snare of the law, the courts, in the web of family history, in all those things whose severest weapon is consistency, and I knew he would not fare well.

"I'd settle."

My father nodded. He pointed the shotgun at the gunnysack of pigeons.

"Better than skeet," he said.

"I'll release them."

"You don't want to shoot? You want, you can go first."

I looked at the gun, resting across my father's lap. I knew no magic inhered in the piece itself, that it was just a shotgun, but even though I could convince myself that the thing housed no resident boogie, I wouldn't touch it.

"I'll just do the birds," I said.

I carried both sacks about fifty yards away, intensely aware that my back was turned to my father. A spot at the base of my neck grew hot. My heart beat in a way that made me conscious of it. I untied the knot on the first sack and gently cradled a pigeon in my palm. I covered its eyes and looked at my father. He nodded. I spun the bird in circles, round and round, and then I set it down. It fell over. The next few moments were kind of vaudevillian. The pigeon flapped its wings, raising a cloud of dust, scooting sideways over the ground, pratfalling, and then it took flight, rising drunkenly in the air, executing a few goofy loops and turns. By instinct the pigeon appeared to know it was supposed to fly, but couldn't figure out the up and down of it. It smashed to the ground, leaden, then rose again. Before it could gain equilibrium and fly level, I heard the deep percussive blast of the shotgun, and the pigeon jerked back, propelled by the impact, and fell like a limp dishrag from the sky. Immediately I grabbed another bird. Its heart raced in my palm. Dad gave the nod. I spun it around and released it, watching as it rose just so far and then exploded in a flak burst of gray feathers. Each time, for the moment I held the bird, I could feel its life, the heart and the breastbones and the soft cooing in its throat, but there really was no moment of decision on my part, no hesitation, as I released the bird. I tossed another into the air, watching it struggle wildly against falling, then rise erratically, lifting above the trees, and get blown out of the sky.

"Take a shot," my dad said.

"No thanks," I said.

He came to me, and we sat down again. He drank from the gin and passed the bottle.

"This used to be open country out here," he said. "But I think we're inside the city limits now. I think we're in the suburbs."

I took a drink, and said, "You know the christening dress? All of us were baptized in that. Mom was, and Grandpa too."

"Yeah, so?"

"Where is it?"

"She'll get an annulment. Everything to nothing in the eyes —"

I interrupted. "But we'll never see it again, right?"

When he didn't answer, I said, "Let's head out."

"There's one more pigeon left."

I folded open the sack and let the bird go. It walked around, head bobbing, among the dead ones.

My father, on Thorazine, always became childlike. He walked in slanted, headlong, stumbling bursts that ended when he smacked into walls or collapsed in a heap on the carpet. He hid in closets, he broke his head open falling down stairs. We cleaned up after him, we mopped piss off the bathroom floor, we helped my mother wipe his muddied ass. At dinner, we wrapped a bedsheet around his neck and spoon-fed him pureed carrots and canned spaghetti and pale green peas we mushed with a fork. We fought over the chance to feed him, played airplane games with the zooming spoon. He babbled and sputtered and sometimes through the Thorazine fog the rudiments of language bubbled up. Once while the nine of us sat at the table, silently eating our dinner, he began to mumble, and we all leaned forward to listen. "Fuck you," he said. "Fuck you. Fuck you. Fuck you." My mother pushed another spoonful of mashed potato in his mouth and it burbled back out in a fuck-you.

As the youngest I was never left alone with my father, never left to care for him by myself — except once, and briefly. Everyone was out and I remember the strangeness of being in the house alone with him. I asked him, did he want to watch TV? When he was crazy, the television ran constantly. I flipped the dial from sports to cartoons to network coverage of the last lunar mission, Apollo 17. Then he spoke — it was a miracle, like hearing a child's first words. He wanted me to go through the house and gather up all the sunglasses I could find. Despite his ongoing bouts of insanity, he was still my father, no crazier than the dads in the Old Testament, and I obeyed him. I thought it was a game. I tore through the house. "Thataboy," he shouted whenever I found a new pair of glasses. I gathered up Jackie's wire rims, a pair of aviators and blocky tortoise shells, the girls' red and yellow and green plastic Disney glasses. Ski goggles, protective eyewear. My father arranged them on the floor, shuffled them one way, then another way, and then he asked, "Who do you think we can call about these glasses?" I said I didn't think there was anyone. And he said, "Well, I guess we're sitting ducks, then. I guess there's no hope. Isn't there anybody we can call?"

This memory came back to me at the open house. My father had put on his good suit and Sunday shoes but perversely decided not to wear his glasses. Immediately he looked lost. He stumbled around the house, filling shallow dishes with salted nuts, setting out a card table with potato chips and pretzels and pop. There were so many things missing from the house, things like family photos and favorite sympathy cards, things that had earned their places on the wall, on the fireplace mantel, simply by virtue of having always been there, that my father seemed spatially confused, and kept rearranging his dishes of nuts, putting them down on the coffee table, then the end table, then setting them back in their original spots.

"Sit down," I said.

"I'm not supposed to be here," my father said. "Cynthia asked me to vacate for a while."

Cynthia, the agent, was openly miffed when she saw my father. She introduced prospective buyers to me and then quickly moved on. I tagged along. She had a proprietary air as she showed the first few strangers through the house. She took a young, childless couple upstairs and showed them the master bedroom. She stood by the window and pointed to the view, the long sloping hill, the mountains in the west, offering this vista as a possibility for the future. We toured the kitchen, the living room. Then we all went downstairs, to the basement. Half of it was unfinished and the other half was paneled in knotty pine. While the Realtor talked about turning the basement into a rumpus room, I lifted the lid of an old Te-Amo cigar box and found some pennies and pen caps, a few buttons, a harmonica, and several hypodermics. When he was fifteen and sixteen, Jackie had been a junkie, and he'd shoot up in the basement. I'd find him downstairs, nodded off, a needle dangling from his arm. It seemed like ages ago now, my childhood. I closed the box.

The most earnest and eager buyers showed up early, followed by a few dreamers who obviously couldn't make a reasonable offer. By afternoon, though, the tone of things changed. I was standing at the picture window when I saw Mrs. Wooley stroll up the walkway. She was wearing a short skirt and heels. She rang the doorbell and I let her in.

"Bobby," she said. "I'm surprised to see you."

She was an intimate of my mother's and had to have known, of course, that I'd left school. She had a daughter my age finishing up at Yale.

"Nice to see you, Mrs. Wooley," I said.

"Call me Lois," she said. "I think you can do that now."

I offered her a drink. She looked at her watch and said, "No, thank you."

She bit her lip, and a little pink came off on her teeth.

"Last time I saw you," she said, "was at the funeral."

"You thinking of buying the house?"

"I was just in the neighborhood."

"Aren't you always? You live across the street."

"Lois, Lois," I heard my father say. He clasped her hand and smiled warmly. "It's been forever. How are you?" He looked down at his feet, and said, "Things have been crazy."

"Yes," Mrs. Wooley said.

Mrs. Kayhew tottered across the street and walked up the stone steps to our porch as if avoiding cracks. And shortly after, Mrs. Greyham followed, along with several other women from the neighborhood. My father greeted each of them with the same warm, somewhat chastened smile and then, like a docent, he led the entire group on a tour of our house. He was especially kind to Mrs. Kayhew, our next-door neighbor. He took her arm in his and guided her up the stairs. Mrs. Kayhew turned her yellow face toward my father, holding it up at a precise angle, as if her blue eyes were pools of water she didn't want to spill.

The little group stood on the upstairs landing. All the bedroom doors were closed, and the thickly coated brown paint gave them a certain feel, as if they'd been sealed shut a long time ago.

My father nudged a crucifix with his foot. He'd knocked it off the wall the day he came home to find my mother gone. The brass Jesus had come unnailed, and was wedged between two spikes in the banister. Mrs. Greyham looked at the cross and then at my father. I waited to hear the lie he would tell.

"I knocked it off the wall," Dad said.

My dad hitched his trousers and bent down on one knee. He picked up the cross and the Jesus and held them, one in each hand, and then tried to fit them together.

He opened his bedroom door, and all the women stepped in. He showed them the deck and the half bath and the big closet still filled with my mother's clothes. The

big king bed still held the outline of my father in the
wrinkled sheets, an intaglio of a head and legs and an arm
stretching out toward the other pillow. He looked down at
the impression, as if he might slip right back into bed,
occupying the mold of himself.

My father offered to make a pot of tea.

"Tea?" I blurted out.

"That's okay," my dad said.

But none of these women had come to see the house,
which was unexceptional; they'd come to see him. They
were ready to leave.

I asked my father if he'd like to have a drink. The
last light faded from the day and the street lamps were
flickering to life. My father seemed dispirited.

"I think I'll just sit," he said. He pointed to his chair
in the living room and then followed his index finger. He
sat down and removed his wing tips, his navy socks, and
began massaging his feet.

"Boy, they're sore," he said, squeezing his toes.

He sat in the dark, very quietly, as if he'd discovered
a still point.

"Any buyers?"

"Huh? Oh, maybe."

I went to the kitchen and fished my dad's last bar-
biturate from the garbage can. I rattled the amber bottle
and popped the top and dry-swallowed the pill. I used to
steal them out of his medicine cabinet all the time. The
thing about barbiturates is they make you feel caressed or
gently held, your skin humming all over with the touch of
a thousand fingers. I sat at the dining table and took apart

Miles's old reel, dabbing drops of Remington gun oil on the pawls, and then went outside and rigged up the fly rod, drawing the line through the guides. I stripped out twenty-five feet of line and began false casting. At first I was out of practice, throwing wide loops that dipped low on the backcast and piled up on the forecast, but with each stroke I made a minor adjustment and soon I could feel the rhythm, marking time. To Mrs. Wooley across the street I might have looked like a man sending semaphore to a distant ship. I worked the line until I was casting forty, fifty feet, and the back-and-forth motion felt substantial, bending the rod down to the butt. I took up a couple of extra coils in my left hand and shot those forward. The line sailed smoothly through the guides and unfurled across the street.

Holding Miles's rod in my hand, I thought of him, my surviving, wrecked brother. A few weeks after he jumped from the Aurora Bridge, I decided, one night, to walk out there. I'm terrified of heights, and I walked slowly out onto the bridge, step by step, my hand rubbing the dirty railing, until I'd made it midway onto the span. My legs weakened, my hands shook and burned with sweat. I had not yet looked down but I didn't need to; the fear rose toward me. I closed my eyes and felt the gritty wind suctioned by oncoming traffic. I heard the clack of tires over the concrete, the screech of a seagull. When I looked down, some three hundred feet, where the black water of Union Bay glinted with city lights, I couldn't move, I froze. My legs wouldn't work. I felt the fall in my stomach, an opening up and a hollowing out. I couldn't move forward up the bridge, or back where I'd come from. I couldn't let go of the rail. I might have been there for an hour, easy, when a woman, out walking her dog, came by. My fear of heights overcame my normal fear of speaking to strangers, and I told her I couldn't move. "I'm afraid," I said, pointing over the edge. She switched the leash to her other hand. "I thought I could cross," I explained. The woman took my hand. She talked us across, I know, because I remember the sound of her voice, but I have no idea what she said, and on the other side of the bridge I thanked her ridiculously, over and over, and the next day I rode the bus back to the bridge to pick up my truck.

My father came out. He was barefoot, but otherwise he still wore the suit. He scratched the back of his hand, and looked over his shoulders at our house. I lifted the line off the street and started casting again.

"I'll never settle," he said.

"Your choice, I guess."

I kept casting, working the rod back and forth, the line flowing gently in watery curls, whispering over our heads.

"It's beautiful," my father said. "Like haiku."

"Let me give it a try," he said.

I let the line fall and stood behind him, closing his hand around the cork, then closing my hand over his.